7

P9-DNL-226

THE VIOLATED

THE VIOLATED

A NOVEL

BILL PRONZINI

B L O O M S B U R Y
NEW YORK · LONDON · OXFORD · NEW DELHI · SYDNEY

Bloomsbury USA
An imprint of Bloomsbury Publishing Plc

1385 Broadway	50 Bedford Square
New York	London
NY 10018	WC1B 3DP
USA	UK

www.bloomsbury.com

BLOOMSBURY and the Diana logo are trademarks of Bloomsbury Publishing Plc

First published 2017

© by the Pronzini-Muller Family Trust 2017

ISBN: HB: 978-1-63286-660-8
ePub: 978-1-63286-662-2

LIBRARY OF CONGRESS CATALOGING-IN-PUBLICATION DATA
Names: Pronzini, Bill, author.
Title: The violated / Bill Pronzini.
Description: First edition. | New York: Bloomsbury USA, 2016.
Identifiers: LCCN 2016025590 | ISBN 9781632866608 (hardcover: alk. paper) |
ISBN 9781632866615 (paperback) | ISBN 9781632866622 (EPUB)
Subjects: | BISAC: FICTION / Crime. | GSAFD: Mystery fiction.
Classification: LCC PS3566.R67 V56 2016 | DDC 813/.54—dc23
LC record available at https://lccn.loc.gov/2016025590

2 4 6 8 10 9 7 5 3 1

Typeset by RefineCatch Limited, Bungay, Suffolk

Printed and bound in the U.S.A. by Berryville Graphics Inc., Berryville, Virginia

To find out more about our authors and books visit
www.bloomsbury.com. Here you will find extracts, author interviews,
details of forthcoming events, and the option to
sign up for our newsletters.

Bloomsbury books may be purchased for business or
promotional use. For information on bulk purchases please contact
Macmillan Corporate and Premium Sales Department at
specialmarkets@macmillan.com.

For Marcia

Crime and the fear of crime have permeated the fabric of American life.

—Warren E. Burger

All human sin seems so much worse in its consequences than in its intentions.

—Reinhold Niebuhr

ACKNOWLEDGMENTS

My thanks once again to Mike White for his help with matters of police procedure and criminal law; and to Barry Malzberg for suggesting a more apt title than my original.

PROLOGUE

The dead man lay faceup on the grassy riverbank, legs together and ankles crossed, arms spread-eagled above his head with palms upturned and fingers curled, in a grotesque parody of the crucifixion. He was positioned closer to the water's edge than to the asphalt path that paralleled the river, the soles of his shoes less than a yard from its thin rind of mud. Early-morning April sunlight laid a pale gold sheen on the waxen features, causing the sightless eyes to shine as if with a faint inner fire. Flies and other insects crawled in the wounds in head and groin, though the blood was dry now.

Two boys on their way through Echo Park for a Saturday morning of fishing saw the body shortly after they emerged from the wooded area above where it lay. They ventured close enough for a clear look, then turned and raced back to the parking lot beyond the picnic area and children's playground, where the older of the two used his cell phone to call 911 as he'd been taught to do in an emergency.

The first patrol unit, responding to the Santa Rita Police Department dispatcher's Code 2, possible 187 radio call, arrived in a little more than five minutes. The officers, Leo Malatesta and John Jablonski, questioned the boys briefly, then followed the route the boys had taken to the riverbank. After a brief visual examination of the corpse, Malatesta, the senior member of the team, told his partner to make sure both boys stayed put in case they were needed for further questioning. He then flipped the switch on the shoulder radio mic velcroed to his uniform epaulet to confirm the 187 and request immediate assistance.

While he waited, Malatesta studied the crime scene. The dead man appeared to have been shot twice, maybe three times, with a handgun of undetermined caliber—a revolver, if the lack of shell casings in the vicinity was any indication. Probably right here on the bank, since there were no drag marks or other indications that the homicide had taken place elsewhere and the victim transported here.

Judging from the dried blood, the state of rigor, and the accumulation of insects, he had been dead since sometime the previous night. On a cold night this time of year, the area would have been deserted after dark. The dew-damp grass was thick and spongy, the ground beneath it fairly solid; you could tell where it had been walked on, but there wouldn't be any clear footprints. Here and there around the body the grass was mashed down but not torn up as it would have been in any kind of struggle or dragging. In addition to the asphalt path above, an irregular, man-made path angled upward through the grass into the line of evergreen trees above, the route the boys had taken. Victim and perp or perps could have used either to get to this point.

There was little chance of anyone having witnessed the crime. This was a sheltered spot, trees hiding the picnic area to the north, more trees growing down close to the water's edge to the south. Malatesta turned toward the river. The recent drought had narrowed it some, but it was still fairly wide here, and brown with silt. It ran in a more or less straight line past the park, then bellied sharply eastward to where it tapered down on its course through the town proper. Farmland lined the far acreage at this point, the few visible buildings too far away for anyone to see over to this bank in the daytime, much less at night.

That was all there was for him to look at and conclude. A careful search of the area and a hands-on search of the corpse was the Investigative Unit's job.

He was still looking out at the river when his partner returned. "Coroner and ambulance on the way," he told Jablonski. "Lieutenant Ortiz and the rest of the IU likewise."

"Chief Kells?"

"Also being notified."

"Kids'll stay put. I got their names and addresses to make sure." Jablonski looked around. "Any sign of the weapon?"

"Not that I could see."

"Thrown in the river. Or else the perp took it away with him." Jablonski moved to where he had a better view of the dead man's face. "You know him, Leo?"

"Don't you?"

"Not with all that blood—" Then, in sudden recognition: "Christ!"

"Yeah," Malatesta said. "It's him, all right. No wonder the shooter put a round or two in his crotch."

"If that's why he was killed."

"Why the hell else? Capped him in his junk first so he'd suffer some, then finished him off."

"Execution-style."

"Not quite. No star-shaped laceration, just powder tattooing. Close range but not a contact wound."

"Mad as hell, whoever pulled the trigger."

"Right."

"Why lay him out like this, I wonder."

Malatesta made no comment.

"Funny," Jablonski said. "Even with the guy's past sex crimes record, the DA wouldn't charge him on account of insufficient evidence. If he'd still been in jail on the other felony rap, this wouldn't've happened."

"Not now, it wouldn't. Not here. Some other time, some other place, maybe."

"You think he was guilty, Leo?"

"Don't you?"

"Bound to be a hell of an uproar whether he was or not. Another media swarm, too."

"Yeah."

"Maybe they'll interview us, put us on TV. First officers on the scene."

Malatesta shrugged. "You go back to the parking lot, Johnny. I'll wait here. Don't let anybody come down except the lieutenant and his crew."

"Right."

Alone again, Malatesta stood over the body and watched the feeding insects. One of the swarm of flies, a big bluebottle with its wings glistening in the pale sunlight, sat on a staring eyeball. Ants moved in a solid line from the torn and bloody crotch across a pant leg and down into the grass.

He spat into the mud rind beyond the up-pointed shoes. "Just what you deserved, you son of a bitch," he said. "Whoever blew you away ought to get a medal."

PART ONE
SATURDAY, APRIL 16

LIANE TORREY

WHEN I OPENED THE door and saw Police Chief Kells and the detective lieutenant, Ortiz, standing on the porch, I knew right away why they were here. The other times they'd come, together and separately, it had been to hound and arrest Martin and search the house and car and question me, but this time it was different, terribly different. I could see it in their faces.

"He's dead, isn't he," I said. "My husband is dead."

Ortiz started to say something, but Kells silenced him with a gesture. "Answer me. Is he dead?"

"Yes," Kells said. "We're sorry, Mrs. Torrey."

No, you're not. You're not one bit sorry, either of you. "How? Where?"

He cleared his throat. "It would be better if we talked inside."

I said, "All right," but I couldn't seem to move. I'd been cold all morning—now my skin felt as if it had been sprayed with dry ice.

The two cops looked at each other. Big men, both of them, Kells fair-haired and slow-speaking, Ortiz dark and sharp-tongued. Neither wore a uniform, now or at any of the other times I'd seen them. The chief's conservative blue suit was rumpled, the knot in his plain tie crooked, as if he'd dressed in a hurry; the lieutenant's gray suit and patterned tie were immaculate. I don't know why I should have noticed any of that now. I hadn't paid attention to how they were dressed the other times.

Kells took a half step forward, tentatively lifting his hand. I thought he was going to touch me, and I couldn't have stood that. I willed myself to turn around, walk back into the house. Slow, heel and toe, my legs so numb I could barely feel myself moving. I heard them come in behind me, one of them close the door. In the living room I lowered myself into one of the Naugahyde chairs. Both men stayed on their feet.

"Would you like a sweater, a blanket?" Kells asked.

The question seemed strange until I realized I was trembling and he'd noticed it. "No. I'm all right. Tell me what happened to Martin."

"He was killed sometime last night."

"Killed. How?"

"Not by accident, I'm afraid."

"How?"

"Shot to death," Ortiz said. He was the blunt one, the angry one who'd given Martin such a hard time. There was an undercurrent of anger in his voice now—he still believed as strongly as ever in Martin's guilt. "In Echo Park, near the river."

Shot . . . murdered. Very little shock in that, almost none. I would have been more surprised to hear that Martin had died in a car wreck or suffered a fatal coronary. "Who shot him?"

"We don't know yet," Kells said. "But we'll find out."

"Will you." It wasn't a question.

"Yes, we will."

"Even if you do, there won't be any justice for my husband."

There was a little silence that Kells seemed to find awkward. He cleared his throat again before he said, "Are you up to answering a few questions, or would you rather we came back later?"

"Tell me something first. Do I have to see the . . . do I have to go look at him?"

"No, it's not required. Your sister or her husband can make the official identification. It might be better if you didn't."

Yes, it would. I didn't want to see Martin for the last time like that, dead. Add that sort of memory to all the other ugly ones. "Then I won't," I said. "Go ahead, ask your questions."

"We're not sure yet exactly when the shooting took place. Sometime last night, after dark."

"Martin had no reason to go to Echo Park after dark."

"Didn't he?" Ortiz said. "At least once?"

Kells gave him a sharp look. I didn't look at him at all.

"It doesn't appear that your husband went to the park voluntarily," Kells said. "At least his car wasn't found in the vicinity, or anywhere else yet. Do you have any idea where he might have gone last evening, who he might have met?"

"No."

"When did you last see him?"

"After dinner. About seven."

"Did he say anything to you before he left?"

"No." Not even good-bye.

Ortiz said, "Closemouthed about everything, as usual."

"Not everything, no." Just the things he thought might hurt me, hurt us. "Protective."

"How's that again?"

"Never mind. It doesn't matter now."

"What kind of mood was he in?"

Restless, uncommunicative, depressed. The way he'd been ever since they arrested him two weeks ago and he was fired from his job because of that and all the suspicion that went with it. But I couldn't tell them that—they would have put the wrong meaning on it again. "No different than usual," I said.

"Taking one of his night drives. Is that what you thought?"

"Yes."

"Always went alone. Never once invited you along."

He preferred to go by himself, it was his way of unwinding so he could sleep. We'd both told Ortiz that before. He didn't believe it, so why say it again?

"But not last night," he said. "There would not have been enough time for a long drive before he was killed."

I had nothing to say to that, either.

"Did he contact you at any time after he left?"

"No. I went to a movie with my sister and I had my phone turned off, but there weren't any voice mail messages. And no call after I got home."

"He didn't usually stay out all night, did he?"

"No."

"Weren't you worried when he didn't come home or call?"

"Yes, I was worried."

"But you didn't report him missing this morning."

"What good would it have done if I had? You'd have just thought he ran away."

"But you didn't think that."

"No, I didn't. He had no reason to run or hide, no matter what you think."

"Mrs. Torrey," Kells said, "did anything . . . well, anything we should know about happen the past few days?"

"Such as what?"

"Someone threatening your husband, or exhibiting hostility toward him."

Two or three anonymous calls. Whispers, stares, glares, pointing fingers whenever people recognized him from his picture in the papers and on TV. Sex offender, suspected rapist. Little gusts of suspicion and hate like a polluted wind. But that wasn't what Kells meant.

"Two days ago," I said, "a man accosted Martin in the parking lot at Safeway."

"Accosted him how? Physically?"

"Not exactly. He called Martin vicious names, spat in his face."

"Threaten him with bodily harm?"

"Not in so many words."

"Do you know the man's name?"

"Yes. Martin worked with him at the brewery. Spivey."

"Jack Spivey," Ortiz said. "Husband of the second assault victim."

"We'll have a talk with him," Kells said. "About last evening, Mrs. Torrey. Did you have visitors or calls while you and your husband were home together?"

"My sister called before dinner, to invite me to the movie." *You need to get out of the house, Liane, take your mind off all the trouble. It's a comedy, supposed to be very funny.* But Holly was wrong, it hadn't been even a little bit funny. "That's all."

There were a few more questions, not many, not important, and then Kells said again that they were sorry for my loss, as if he honestly meant it, and then they left me alone.

I sat in the silence. Once I closed my eyes, but I didn't like the dark, I'd come to hate the dark, and I opened them again right away. I knew I ought to get up and call Holly and Nick, let them know what had happened, but again I seemed to have lost the will and the ability to move. Frozen in the chair. Trembling inside and out. Thinking: *He's dead, he's gone, I'll never see him again.* Thinking: *God help me, maybe it's better this way. Better for both of us.*

I wondered how long it would be before I was able to cry for him. Or if I'd ever be able to cry at all.

GRIFFIN KELLS

NEITHER ROBERT NOR I spoke for a while after we left the Torrey house. We'd come in my cruiser, and now that the task of informing and questioning the widow was done, I was a little sorry I hadn't come alone. The unpleasant duty would have been less difficult, less stressful, if Ortiz hadn't been present.

When I turned onto Hillsdale Avenue, I said to break the silence, "You were a little rough on Mrs. Torrey."

"You know why."

"Still. Recent widow, grieving. She didn't have anything to do with the assaults, even if her husband did."

"Except possibly concealing evidence or guilty knowledge."

We'd been over that before. I repeated what I'd said previously, that she didn't strike me as the type.

"She stood by him the entire time in Ohio," Robert said. "Moved out here with him, arranged his bail on the felony charge, kept defending him."

"Love and loyalty don't have to mean knowledge or complicity. Assuming Torrey was guilty of more than just failure to register as a nonviolent sex offender."

"Short step between nonviolent and violent. He was guilty, all right."

I wished I were similarly convinced, but no evidence supported Robert's conviction. "No attacks since you first latched onto him," I pointed out.

"Only a little more than two weeks, and his MO was one assault per month. He wasn't stupid. Now that he's dead, there won't be any more."

We lapsed into silence again. Robert was a good cop, a good man, but he had a stubborn streak and there was no point in arguing with him on the subject. He also had a constant need to prove himself, despite an exemplary record and one of the top ratings in the California Peace Officers Association's highly specialized "advanced officer" training course. It might have had something to do with his heritage, not that there was any obvious prejudice in Santa Rita against Latinos or any other ethnic group; another IU officer, Sergeant Al Bennett, was African-American, one of our patrol officers was Chinese and two others Latino, there was a black woman on the city council, a Latino on the Planning Commission.

Or maybe it was just part of Robert's DNA; in addition to being stubborn he was intense, hardworking, dedicated, ambitious. Hard to judge exactly what drove him because it was not the kind of thing you could discuss with him. He didn't invite personal confidences. Not that he was aloof or standoffish, just that he was all-business in the work environment. He reserved his private life for family and friendships outside the department.

When he got his teeth into something, he was like a dog with a bone: he wouldn't let go until it was finished to his satisfaction. He'd had his teeth deep into the serial rapes from the beginning, and not only because of his position as SRPD's head investigator. He was a staunch Catholic with a strong sense of moral rectitude. And he had two teenage daughters and an attractive wife. Even though he'd never said so, I suspected he was dogged by the possibility, however remote, that one of them might wind up defiled, beaten, humiliated, like the four victims to date.

His belief that Martin Torrey was the rapist was based on gut instinct, the thin circumstantial evidence we'd gathered from the crime scenes and victims' testimony, and the facts that Torrey had a sex-crimes conviction in Ohio and had concealed that from both the California Department of Justice and his employer. But the Ohio conviction wasn't for rape, attempted rape, or molestation; he'd been caught masturbating while watching a woman taking a bath and subsequently confessed to three other incidents of voyeurism—aberrant misdemeanors he professed to be deeply ashamed of. Nine months in a psychiatric facility had cured him of the compulsion, according to official reports from his attending physicians. Robert had come down hard on him nonetheless, and harder still once word of his past offenses came through NICS.

Only time would tell if Robert was right and Torrey's death marked the end of the serial assaults. Meanwhile, the possibility of more attacks would continue to cause tension, fear, anger, in the community. Torrey's murder solved nothing, served only to make a bad situation worse.

The sexual assaults already had the mayor, the city council, the media, and citizens groups up in arms and clamoring for results. "Justice" dispensed by some fool with a gun and a bellyful of rage might meet with the approval of some, but it set a dangerous precedent. Guilty until proven innocent. Condemned without just cause. That kind of mentality was intolerable.

"Jack Spivey," I said. "You spent more time with him than I did. He strike you as the type to take the law into his own hands?"

"He's full of *machismo*," Robert said. "And very angry at what was done to his wife."

At least a borderline racist, too, judging from his open hostility toward Robert the one time I'd met him. And a hunter and gun collector—rifles, shotguns, handguns, all legally registered. One of his handguns, a .38 S&W, had been stolen after the assault on Ione Spivey. It had been kept in a nightstand between their twin beds, and the perp spotted it when she tried to get at it during the act. More fuel for a killing rage in a hothead like Jack Spivey.

"Well, it'll make our lives easier if he's the shooter," I said. "Too many other possibles if he's not. Husbands, boyfriends, brothers, other relatives of the victims. Or just some crazy who's seen too many Clint Eastwood movies."

"If it's a man."

I'd had that thought, too. "Yeah. But very few women are hard-core vigilantes, if that's the motive. And they tend to be more impulsive than men when it comes to a revenge killing. Shoot their victims on the spot, quick, instead of taking or luring them out to a place like Echo Park."

"Unless Echo Park had some special significance."

"Such as?"

"The first victim was assaulted there."

"That's a possibility," I admitted.

"There's another," Robert said. "A fifth rape attempt and Torrey picked the wrong victim, one who was armed for self-protection."

"Then where's his car? And how did he get to the park?"

"Grabbed the victim somewhere else and forced her to drive him there."

"That doesn't match his MO," I reminded him. "On-the-spot attacks in each of the other three assaults, and all in different locales."

"Torrey could have reverted to the park again for number five," he said. "How can we know what goes on in the head of a serial rapist?"

We were entering the historic part of downtown now, past the hundred-year-old brick-and-false-front buildings that flanked the main drag. The cherry trees spaced along the Donner Street sidewalks were in full bloom, a sea of white. Usually spring was my favorite time of year. New growth everywhere, the eastern and far-western hills still bright green despite the ongoing drought—just enough rain this year to keep them that way into April. The streets seemed less crowded than usual for a Saturday, or maybe that was just my imagination. They wouldn't stay that way once word of the murder spread. The fourth, most violent rape and Torrey's subsequent arrest had brought media not only from Riverton, the county seat, and other nearby towns, but from Sacramento and San Francisco. The Torrey homicide would bring them flocking back. And once again I'd have microphones stuck in my face, questions hurled at me, statements to make.

Santa Rita used to be a quiet town. Somewhat off the beaten track, not much in the way of tourist attractions except for boating, fishing, hiking, and hunting in the nearby foothills, the economy supported mainly by agriculture, Santa Rita Feed and Grain, Soderholm Brewery. Somewhat old-fashioned in attitude as well as architecture, with a real small-town sense of community—active Chamber of Commerce and Rotary, parades on Veterans Day and the Fourth of July, charity fund-raisers at the community center, carnivals and other events at the fairgrounds, Little League baseball and adult softball leagues, a Boys & Girls Club, a little theater group. Better-than-average schools. Two public swimming pools. A downtown park with a bandstand, Echo Park with its picnic areas and limited river access. All in all a good place to live, raise a family. Raise my family, if I could finally talk Jenna into starting one.

Before the sexual predator, whoever the hell he was, started his reign of terror, there was relatively little crime. Drug-related offenses, mainly— scattered incidents of possession with and without intent to sell, small-time marijuana-growing, a hash-oil explosion a year ago that luckily hadn't resulted in any casualties. Otherwise the usual random assortment of DUIs and DDs and bar brawls and domestic-abuse cases; petty theft, burglaries, other nonviolent felonies. Very little of the gang violence you have in other small Northern California towns with a population of around fifty thousand; what there was in the county was concentrated in Riverton, which was more than twice our size. And almost no homicides. Until Martin Torrey's body was found this morning, there'd been only two during my seven years as chief of police, one a domestic stabbing and the other a shooting involving drugs.

My shoulder radio crackled as we crossed the River Street bridge. Sergeant Eversham notifying me that Mayor Delahunt wanted to see me in his office ASAP. Damn. My relationship with Delahunt had been adversarial ever since I was hired by the city council over his handpicked candidate, Captain Frank Judkins, and the lack of progress on the assaults, for which the mayor blamed me, had strained the relationship even more. The Torrey homicide would have him in a dither. I was in no mood for a session with him, but I couldn't very well avoid him. I said to tell His Honor I'd be there in twenty minutes or so.

"I'll have a talk with Jack Spivey," Robert said when I signed off.

"Better take Al Bennett or Karl Simms along." They were the other two male members of the IU. The fourth, Sergeant Susan Sinclair, worked gender-sensitive crimes and served as victims' advocate.

"Not necessary. I can handle Spivey."

Robert being stubborn again. "Okay," I said, "but go easy on him unless he gives you serious trouble." The SRPD was under a public microscope these days, like so many law enforcement agencies nation-wide. The last thing we needed was a lawsuit for police harassment.

"He won't give me any trouble."

"Let's hope not. Check in with me after you see him."

City Hall was just up ahead now, an old adobe-brick building that needed retrofitting if the city council could ever find enough money for the job. The relatively new PD building, beige-colored plaster over rein-forced cinder block, stood at an angle behind it. Nearly twice the size of the old one, it had up-to-date communications equipment, more rooms, a small but well-outfitted lab, and two additional holding cells. There was a shared parking lot between the two buildings and a fenced-off security section next to the station.

I pulled into the marked chief's space, next to where Robert's cruiser was parked, then walked over to City Hall. On the way, I thought wryly that no matter how things turned out with Jack Spivey, Robert's meeting with him was liable to be less disagreeable than mine with our esteemed mayor.

HUGH DELAHUNT

I HAVE ALWAYS MADE an effort to get along with the media. You can't have a future in politics unless you get the newshawks on your side and keep them there. There are ways to do that, little tricks you learn early on. Always be prepared, no matter what subject is on the table. Always be polite, even in contentious situations. Give straightforward answers to the questions you're willing to address and be careful how you sidestep the ones you're not. Never lie or conceal anything unless you're absolutely sure you won't get caught out.

The same methods apply in dealing with the voters individually, in small groups, in public forums. Some are knowledgeable, but a high percentage are herd followers; they believe most if not all of what they see on TV or read in newspapers and on the Internet and vote accordingly. Keeping the media on Hugh Delahunt's side is essential. It was how I got elected mayor, and it was how I was going to be elected to the county board of supervisors next year, and, if all went according to plan, to the state assembly in the not-too-distant future.

All of that sounds crass and self-serving, I know. But it doesn't mean I don't care about the people and the city of Santa Rita. I'm proud to say I devote considerable time and effort to getting things done to improve the common good. You have to be hard-nosed to accomplish those objectives, and to make more political hay doing so. I can honestly say that I have been a strong, forceful leader during my two terms. Santa Rita is a better place to live since I took office. Or it was until these goddamn rapes threw everything into turmoil.

It certainly isn't my fault Chief Kells and his minions are ineffectual bumblers. Yet I'm forced to endure almost as much flak as they are, as if I were also responsible. And already I was being subjected to more, even though the murder of Martin Torrey had happened less than twenty-four hours ago and I had known about it for less than four.

Not flak from the media at large, thanks to my cordial relations with them. No, all the heat past and present was coming from the one man I hadn't been able to win over no matter how hard I'd tried. For some benighted reason, Ted Lowenstein had taken a dislike to me from the minute he bought the *Santa Rita Clarion* three years ago, and he has been a splinter in my ass ever since. Critical editorials, snide remarks in news stories and at city council meetings, and all for the flimsiest of reasons. Party advisers keep reassuring me that his attacks haven't done me any real harm, and I'm sure they're right. Still, the *Clarion* is distributed and read countywide, not just in Santa Rita, and Lowenstein also makes it available on his website and on a blog he writes. Some of the herd-following voters are bound to be swayed by all the unfair sniping—not enough to cost me the supervisor's seat in the next election, surely, but it makes me uncomfortable nonetheless.

Lowenstein's harassment would increase the longer the rapes and now this revenge or vigilante murder went unsolved. He had made that plain enough through innuendo when he showed up at my office ten minutes after I did. If I had refused his request for an interview, he would have found a way to turn it against me. So here he was, sitting across my desk from me in one of the ridiculous Hawaiian shirts he favored, his skinny legs crossed, his sparse brindle hair sticking up every which way as usual. Those shirts and that seldom-combed hair and his confrontational atti-tude explained why he was long divorced and had never remarried. What was puzzling was how a man who looked like him could have fathered such an attractive daughter. Angela Lowenstein, at least, had none of the same axes to grind at my expense. None that were apparent, anyway.

I forced myself to be pleasant and cooperative, to the point of allowing

Lowenstein to record our conversation. "Come on now, Ted," I said, smiling, "tell me how you found out about the murder so quickly. I was only informed myself a short while ago."

"I have my sources. As you well know."

"In the police department, I suppose."

"Privileged information."

"Well, in any case there's nothing I can tell you. Chief Kells is the man you should be talking to. He's due here any minute, as a matter of fact."

"Good. Meanwhile, Mr. Mayor, what's your initial reaction to the shooting?"

"Outrage, of course."

"Really? I would have thought you'd be pleased."

"Pleased? Why in heaven's name would I be pleased about the first homicide in Santa Rita in three years?"

"It solves the serial rapes, doesn't it?"

"If Martin Torrey was guilty, it does. Had there been enough proof to bring charges against him, District Attorney Conrad would have done so."

"But you do believe he was the rapist."

"My personal feelings are irrelevant. This is America—a man is innocent until proven guilty."

"Mayor Hugh Delahunt, master of the evasive response and the appropriate cliché."

I refused to dignify that snotty slur with a response.

"'Innocent until proven guilty.' You've been heard to say differently here and there in private," Lowenstein said. "My sources again."

My smile dipped slightly; I restored it before I said, "Your sources are inaccurate and malicious."

"On the contrary. You were heard to state more than once before witnesses that Torrey was guilty as hell. To Craig Soderholm, among others. Your brother-in-law didn't waste any time firing Torrey."

"Are you suggesting *I* had a hand in that?"

"Didn't you?"

Well, I did, as a matter of fact. With complete justification. Craig is not decisive and is inclined to give undue benefit of doubt. Public feeling had been running high against Torrey, guilty of rape or not, since his arrest on the other felony charge, and allowing him to remain on the brewery payroll would have reflected badly on the company, the family, and me.

"Well, Mr. Mayor?"

I smoothed my neatly trimmed mustache, a habit of mine while framing answers to certain questions. "Torrey was let go," I said slowly, "because of his failure to register as a convicted sex offender—"

"A minor felony given the nature of his Ohio crimes."

"—and for deliberately lying about his past criminal record on his employment application."

"So in effect you're saying Soderholm Brewery's personnel department was lax in not checking his background."

"That's not what I'm saying at all. He was hired as a deliveryman, a low-level position, on the recommendation of his brother-in-law. It isn't always considered necessary to check an individual's background or additional references in such cases."

"May I quote you on that?"

"No, you may not. Now if you have no more questions—"

"Oh, I have quite a few more questions. Do you think Torrey's murder was motivated by revenge? Or is it a case of vigilantism—a misguided citizen eliminating the man he believes, as you do, to have been the serial rapist?"

"If I were you," I said, smiling with difficulty now, "I wouldn't equate my feelings with those of a murderer in print."

"I won't. I know the libel laws better than you. Are you going to answer my question?"

"Yes, by saying I refuse to speculate on motive until more facts have been gathered. And you *can* quote me on that."

Lowenstein shrugged his scrawny shoulders. "I've been given to understand there are no suspects in the shooting as yet. True?"

"You'll have to ask Chief Kells."

"Word also is that Torrey was shot three times, once in the temple and twice in the groin, the groin shots obliterating the poor bugger's privates. Can you confirm that?"

"No, I can't." A brief mental image of obliterated privates made me wince slightly in spite of myself. "You'll have to ask Chief Kells."

"Has the weapon been recovered? Or at least the caliber identified?"

"You'll have to ask Chief Kells."

Lowenstein chuckled. "You don't think the chief and Robert Ortiz will solve this crime, do you?"

"They had four months to satisfactorily solve the assaults and failed to do so."

"I'll take that as a yes. So you're still of the opinion that outside help is necessary, despite the fact that all the crimes were committed within the Santa Rita city limits."

"Of course I am. That has been my stated opinion all along."

"But outside help was brought in, to no avail. Or have you forgotten that Kells asked for and was given aid and advice from a state expert on sex crimes? Or that both DA's and county sheriff's investigators were brought in at your insistence, the result of which was a jurisdictional wrangle that hindered rather than benefited the investigation?"

"I have no comment on that."

"No comment. The politician's favorite hiding place."

"You know, Ted"—I still managed to smile—"sometimes you sorely try my patience."

"Fools and political hacks try mine."

The intercom on my desk buzzed. A good thing, too, or I might have lost a little of my cool and said something he could use against me. "Yes, Vernon?" Vernon Nichols, my administrative assistant.

"Chief Kells is here."

"Fine. Send him right in."

Kells came in looking as if he'd slept in his suit. I had long since given up trying to convince him to wear his gold-braid uniform daily instead of only at public functions, or at least to openly display his badge instead of keeping it pinned inside his suit coat. But it annoyed me that he failed to dress himself more neatly. He claimed that he couldn't help it, he was one of those men possessed by invisible gremlins who rumpled him up (his idea of a joke) five minutes after he put on a freshly pressed suit and laundered shirt. Perhaps so, but a sloppy-looking police chief sets a bad example. It reflects poorly on the city, and on me when we share a podium.

Initially, I had opposed his hiring. My choice had been Frank Judkins, no genius, either, but a political ally who deserved the promotion after more than three decades on the force. But the majority of city council members felt that his record was lackluster and that new, younger blood was needed. Kells had been only thirty-five at the time, and while his record in Fresno had been exemplary for the most part, his lack of experience at the administrative level and his nonaggressive methods militated against him in my view. While he had done an adequate if lackluster job until four months ago, he lacked the capability to cope with a major crime wave. He should have been removed by now and Judkins installed in his place, but again the majority of council members disagreed. So did Lowenstein, of course; he was one of Kells's strongest backers. The devil with Lowenstein.

One of Kells's eyebrows lifted when he saw the editor. I said before either of them could speak, "Mr. Lowenstein was just about to leave. Ted, if you'll wait in the outer office, you can talk to the chief when he has finished briefing me."

He ignored me. "Is there anything sensitive or private in your preliminary report that I shouldn't know about or print?" he asked Kells.

"No, not really. Preliminary, as you said."

"Then I'll stay. No point in you wasting your time repeating yourself." He waggled his cell phone in my direction. "You don't mind if I record this conversation as well, do you?"

Of course I minded. I could have made an issue of it, but that was what he wanted me to do—provoke him so he'd have more ammunition for one of his sniping editorials. I said, "As you wish," through another thin smile, then put my eyes on Kells and kept them there. "There has been no arrest yet, I take it."

"No."

"Suspects?"

"No. We've only just begun investigating."

"This is another high-priority case, Chief. You know that as well as I do. I'll expect you and your officers to apprehend the murderer without undue delay."

Lowenstein made a sound that might have been a stifled laugh. One corner of Kells's mouth twitched as he said, "Yes, sir." I knew he disapproved of me as much as I did of him, though unlike Lowenstein, he had always been civil even when we were at loggerheads.

"Go ahead with your report."

There really wasn't much to it. He confirmed that Martin Torrey had been shot three times, once in the left temple, twice in the groin, all at close range. The weapon had not been recovered. None of the bullets had exited the body, the one in the head having apparently lodged against bone, but from the size of the wounds and the amount of damage, the weapon was probably one of the smaller calibers. Based on rigor and livor mortis, the coroner had estimated the time of death at between nine P.M. and midnight; the county's forensic pathologist, Ed Braverman, would be able to narrow that down somewhat when he finished his autopsy. The body had already been released for transport to the central morgue in Riverton, with a request made for priority handling.

Joe Bloom, the Investigation Unit's evidence technician, had found nothing at the scene that might help identify the killer. Torrey's car, a late-model Toyota Camry, had not been found in Echo Park or anywhere else so far, which indicated a likelihood that he had been taken to the park by the person or persons responsible. Kells and Lieutenant Ortiz had notified and interviewed Torrey's wife, who had had nothing pertinent to tell them.

"She may have been lying or withholding information," I said.

"I don't think so, Mayor. I didn't get that impression."

"Impressions are not always reliable."

"Neither are clichés," Lowenstein said in his snotty way.

Kells said, "I don't see that she has any reason to lie."

"She would if she knew her husband was the rapist."

"While he was still alive, yes. Now . . . I just don't think so. She has every reason to want his killer found as much as we do."

"Keep an eye on her just the same."

Lowenstein uncrossed his legs and got slowly to his feet. He said to Kells, "I'm wondering if there might be a witness out there somewhere, somebody who happened to be near Echo Park when Torrey and his killer arrived there. The next issue of the *Clarion* isn't due out until Tuesday, but I can post an appeal on our website and my blog."

"I was about to make the same suggestion."

"As was I," I said, though I hadn't been. "When the TV people arrive and request interviews, Chief Kells and I will make the same appeal. Many more people will be reached that way."

Kells said, "There's one more thing you can do, Ted. Check your files for any particularly angry or threatening communications the *Clarion* received since Torrey first came under suspicion."

"I don't recall any. But, yes, of course I'll check."

"If there's nothing more right now, Mayor," Kells said to me, "I'll get back to work."

"Go ahead. We'll confer again later." I added meaningfully, "Just the two of us."

Lowenstein said he would be on his way, too. Finally. But of course he had to have the last word. "Be sure to read my posts tonight, Mayor. I'm sure you'll find them interesting."

I smiled at him. *Drop dead, you little prick,* I thought.

IONE SPIVEY

I WAS WORKING IN the garden when Lieutenant Ortiz came. Weeding and planting more than my usual amount of annuals and perennials—pansies, zinnias, marigolds, begonias, tea roses. Come June, they would add a lot of bright color to the front and backyards.

If only I could make myself care the way I used to.

Maybe I would by June, maybe all the pretty blossoms would cheer me by then, but the way I felt now I wasn't too hopeful. The garden didn't seem important anymore. Planting the flowers was just something to do, a way to keep my mind as well as my hands occupied. And the house . . . I didn't feel the same about the house at all. I wished we could sell it, move somewhere else, but Jack said no, that wouldn't solve anything. Besides, we'd put a lot of time and money into it, and even though it was a seller's market right now, we wouldn't get enough out of it to buy another nice place in a neighborhood close to Timmy's school. Jack's right, I know he is. But after what happened that terrible night three months ago—

No. I mustn't think about that night, I must learn to block it out as if it had never happened. It was the only way my mind could heal as completely as my body had. Policewoman Sinclair's advice, Dr. Adamson's advice, Reverend Melrose's advice, Jack's advice, my folks' advice. Good advice.

But it's so hard *not* to remember. Some days the mental wall I put up keeps the memories out, but other days, particularly when I'm in the bedroom, it crumbles and lets flashes come through . . . the helplessness, the pain, the violation, the terror. Those memories won't always haunt me this way. I have to believe that one day I'll be able to live my old life again, a normal life . . . have normal feelings, normal relations.

Jack's been patient with me, more patient than I ever thought he could be. He's a gruff man by nature and he loses his temper easily, not that he's ever laid a hand on me or Timmy. He's a good provider, too. Puts in long hours driving for Soderholm Brewery, like the overnight haul he was on the night Timmy stayed over with the Peterson boy and I was alone in the house—

No.

But underneath, Jack's still so angry. I can see it in his eyes, feel it like little pulses of heat when he's near me. He's having as much trouble coping as I am. As much trouble healing. He doesn't like to leave me alone at night now—he swapped with one of the other drivers so he won't have to make any more overnight hauls, and he won't let Timmy sleep away from home. I told him we can't put our lives on hold, keep living in fear, and finally he agreed I was right. Still, he insists that whenever he's not here after dark, I keep all the doors and windows locked and not answer the doorbell if it rings and keep the little .32 purse gun he bought for me close by. Better safe than sorry again.

Neither of us will be the same until they arrest the man who hurt me and those other poor women, lock him up in prison. Jack still thinks it's Martin Torrey, and he's mad at the police for letting him out of jail. I want it to be Torrey, too, but when they had me listen to him say some of the rapist's ugly words, I just couldn't be sure it was the same voice. The other women couldn't be sure, either. It might be that the ski mask distorted his voice during the attacks, but it could also be he's not the right man . . .

All of that was going through my mind when I heard the police car pull up in front, then saw Lieutenant Ortiz get out and come through the gate. Jack says he wishes a white cop was in charge of the investigation instead of a Mexican, but I don't see what difference that would make. Ortiz wouldn't be a lieutenant or command the Investigative Unit if he wasn't good at his job. I liked him, even if Jack didn't.

I hoped he hadn't come to ask again if I'd remembered anything more about the attack, a tiny detail I might have forgotten or blocked out. I'd told him I would let him know right away if I did. But the truth was, I hadn't tried very hard. Thinking too much about that awful night made me physically ill.

I set down the trowel and stood up, brushing dirt off my gloved hands. "Good afternoon, Mrs. Spivey," he said. Polite as always. But he had kind of an intense look today, as if he was upset about something. "Is your husband home? I'd like to speak to him."

"No, he's not. He and Timmy went quail hunting."

"What time do you expect them back?"

"I don't know, probably not until late afternoon. Is there anything I can help you with?"

"Was he home last night?"

"Jack? No, he wasn't. He went bowling. The Soderholm team in the Friday Night Scratch league."

"What time did he leave the house?"

"Around seven."

"And what time did he return?"

"I'm not sure. After eleven sometime . . . I was in bed asleep by then. Why are you asking about last night? Has something happened?"

"Yes. Martin Torrey was shot to death last night in Echo Park."

It took a few seconds for me to process that. No wonder the lieutenant looked upset. "Martin Torrey . . . my God. Was it because he . . . of what happened to me and the other women . . . ?"

"It may have been."

"You don't know who shot him?"

"Not yet."

I had a sudden sick feeling in the pit of my stomach. "Oh, Lord, you don't think it was Jack? Is that why you want to talk to him?"

"We're talking to everyone connected with the assaults."

"It wasn't Jack. He wouldn't kill anyone. He went bowling last night, I told you that."

"I still need to speak to him."

"Well . . . we have dinner around seven. You could come back then."

"I'll call first, to make sure he's home."

When the lieutenant drove away I went into the house, into Jack's den—his man cave, he calls it. The cabinet where he keeps his hunting rifles and his pistols was locked as always. I looked through the glass doors. The pistols were all there, all except the LaserMax he'd put in the bedroom nightstand to replace the revolver the rapist stole. Well, of course they were. Why had I even bothered to look?

It wasn't Jack. He wouldn't kill anyone.

Well, animals and birds, yes. Deer and squirrels and rabbits and ducks and quail. And now he was turning Timmy into a hunter, even though the boy was only ten. To my mind that was too young for blood sports. He seemed to enjoy it more than he should, too. But Jack would never harm a human being unless he was forced to, in self-defense. Never.

Only he'd said more than once that if he knew for sure who raped me, he'd kill the bastard. Blow his brains out and to hell with the consequences.

Oh, but he didn't mean it. It was just his pent-up anger talking. And anyway, he was bowling when Martin Torrey was killed, wasn't he?

I went back outside long enough to pick up my trowel and the few plants I hadn't yet put into the ground. I didn't feel like gardening anymore. Clouds had blotted out the sun and a wind had come up and everything had a gray, cold look now. Even the early-blooming pansies and begonias and marigolds I'd planted didn't seem to have much color anymore.

HOLLY DEXTER

NICK STARTED IN AGAIN as soon as Liane phoned with the horrible news about Martin. I couldn't believe it—the same old whiny complaints when we'd just been blindsided. "Why did they have to move out here? Why couldn't they have stayed in Ohio or gone some other damn place?"

"For God's sake," I snapped at him, "don't you even care that Marty's dead, that some crazy person *murdered* him? That my poor sister's all alone and suffering?"

"Of course I care. But he wouldn't be dead if you hadn't encouraged them to come to Santa Rita. And we wouldn't be out fifteen hundred dollars that now we'll never get back."

"What's the matter with you? How can you think of money at a time like this?"

"I can't help it. We're barely making ends meet as it is. Might as well have flushed that fifteen hundred down the sewer."

"And it's all my fault, right?" I was getting my coat out of the hall closet. "The move, the money, everything."

"I didn't say that. But you insisted we loan it to them—"

"Where else were they going to get it? A thousand was all they had to put up for Marty's bail."

"Allan Zacks offered to loan her the full amount, didn't he? But, oh no, she wouldn't take money from a well-off dentist, just from her poor family."

"Allan's not well-off, he only has a small practice. And it wasn't Liane who said no, it was Marty. He didn't want her beholden to the man she works for."

"Then she should've let him stay in jail."

"He couldn't bear being locked up again as it was, you know that."

"Yeah, well, if he hadn't been afraid to register when he first got here, he wouldn't have been locked up. The cops couldn't prove he had anything to do with the rapes."

"The brewery wouldn't have hired him if he'd registered, even with you sponsoring him. Nobody else would have, either."

"It's a wonder Craig Soderholm didn't fire me, too, when he found out. With my luck, he may still give me the boot."

"Are you coming with me or not?" I had my coat on and my purse in hand. "Liane needs all the comfort and support she can get right now."

"I know it. I'm coming."

We went out and got into the Subaru. Nick wouldn't let me drive, as usual when we went somewhere together. Man's job. Phooey.

"Marty didn't commit those rapes," I said.

"You keep saying that. Trying to convince me or yourself?"

"I'm convinced. Aren't you?"

"I don't think he did it, no."

"He simply wasn't capable of that kind of thing."

"None of us thought he was capable of peeping in windows and jerking off in the bushes, either."

"God, you can be crude. He was sick, he had urges he couldn't control, but he never hurt any of those women in Massillon. The doctors said he was cured when they let him out of the hospital."

"All right."

"And don't say it's funny that women started being raped in Santa Rita six months after he came here."

"I wasn't going to."

"Coincidence, that's all. Stupid goddamn coincidence."

"Okay, okay. I'm on your side here."

"Not mine, Liane's. When we get there, don't say anything to upset her any more than she already is."

"I won't. Christ, you really think I'm that insensitive?"

No, I just think you're an asshole sometimes.

When we got to Liane's small rented house on Grove Street, four or five people were hanging around in front gawking. Nick said, "*They're* the insensitive ones," and he was right. Bad news spreads fast in small towns and brings that type out like roaches smelling spoiled food.

None of them said anything to Nick or me as we went up to the door, and a good thing or I'd have told them what I thought of them. The door was locked, but I didn't want to ring the bell and I had the spare key Liane gave me. I let us in, calling her name.

"In the living room."

The same flat, empty voice as on the phone. She looked empty, too, slumped in one of the chairs, all pale and shaky. I sat on the chair arm, wrapped her in a tight embrace. She just sat there, limp—it was like hugging a rag doll.

"I'm so sorry, honey." It was all I could think of to say, the same thing I'd said on the phone.

She didn't answer, just nodded. Looking at her, I felt tears well up. But her eyes were dry. Well, I could understand that. She'd cried so much and so often for Marty that there just weren't any more tears left in her, not even for this final hurt.

I drew back and took hold of her hands. They were cold as ice. Nick was just standing there with his fat face hanging out. I told him to bring the afghan from the couch, and I wrapped it around Liane. He mumbled something that was meant to be comforting and patted her shoulder like you'd pat a dog. My big, strong husband. Totally useless in a crisis.

I started to get up. "I'll make you something hot to drink. Coffee or tea . . ."

"No, don't bother."

"Something stronger," Nick said. "Brandy, scotch."

"I don't want anything."

"I could use a drink myself. Holly?"

"No."

He shuffled off into the kitchen. I rubbed Liane's hands, trying to warm them. That vacant look in her eyes . . . God, how awful it must be to lose in such a cruel way the man you loved, even a man with Marty's problems and all the heartache he caused her. As much as Nick could irritate me, as much as I felt like slapping him silly sometimes, he'd been mine for better or worse for fourteen years. I couldn't imagine how I'd feel if he suddenly died, violently or any other way. Didn't want to imagine it.

"Liane, honey, you should get into bed." Her hands still had no warmth and I could feel her shivering. "Come on, let me help you."

She didn't argue. I got her up on her feet.

"Nick!"

He came in with a glass in his hand. Straight scotch, from the look of it.

"Help me with Liane."

For once he didn't have to be told something twice; he set his glass down and took hold of Liane's other arm, and together we slow-walked her into the bedroom. I shooed him out and got Liane's clothes off and her into bed. The way she looked up at me with those big, empty eyes was heartbreaking.

The doorbell chimes sounded as I was pulling the down comforter up around her chin. Damn! One of those idiots outside, or the police again, or, worse, one of the media pests already. The bell didn't go off again, so Nick must have gone to the door. If he had any sense left, he'd send whoever it was away quick.

But he didn't. I patted Liane's hand and went out into the living room and heard the sound of voices in the hallway, Nick's and another man's. My anger rising, I hurried out there, but when I saw who the man was, the anger faded. Allan Zacks. It was all right for Nick to have let him in.

"Oh," I said, "hello, Allan."

"Holly. I just heard about Martin."

"One of his patients called him up and told him," Nick said.

I gave him a look. Allan was *our* dentist, too, now—I'd switched us over when Liane got the job as his hygienist.

"It must have been a terrible shock to Liane," Allan said. "How is she bearing up?"

"Numb right now. I just got her into bed."

"She'll be all right?"

"I think so. After she's had some rest."

"I won't disturb her. I probably shouldn't have come rushing over, but I was afraid she might be alone. I should have realized you'd be here."

"Yes, she called me right after the police left."

"Chief Kells and that detective lieutenant, Ortiz," Nick said unnecessarily. "They're the ones who told her."

"You'll be staying with her?" Allan asked me.

"For as long as she needs me."

He nodded. "It's a relief to know she's in good hands. If there's anything I can do . . ."

"Not just now, Allan, thanks."

"Then I'll be going." He paused with his hand on the doorknob. "But I'd like to come back tomorrow, if you think Liane would want to see me."

"Of course she would."

"I'll call first." Then he was gone.

A nice man, Allan. Handsome, too, tall and slim, eyes like chips of green jade. Normally I don't care for full beards on a man, but his was a beautifully shaped dark brown. Nick had been fairly good-looking once, before he put on twenty pounds and developed that grating whine in his voice, and I still loved him, but if I'd had a choice between him and Allan fourteen years ago, there wasn't much doubt which one I'd have picked.

I wondered just how Allan felt about Liane. If his concern went deeper than that of employer and friend. Martin had once said, a little jealously, that he sensed Allan was smitten with her. She pooh-poohed that, saying he'd never come on to her, always been a perfect gentleman, but judging from the way I'd seen him look at her now and then, I suspected there was more than a little truth in the notion.

Well, for her sake I hoped he was smitten and that he'd do something about it eventually. With Marty gone and that part of her life over, she'd need a strong, caring man to build a new life with. And there wasn't a better one around than Dr. Allan Zacks.

TED LOWENSTEIN

FROM CITY HALL I went straight to the *Clarion* offices on Beech Street, six blocks away. Usually only a few of the two dozen staff members come in on Saturdays; today, the breaking story had drawn several. Tyler James, my managing editor, was already working on the front-page layout for Tuesday's print edition. John Nichols, the best of our field reporters, Phil Goldstein, our part-time photographer, and even Royce Smith, the young interim sports reporter, were there.

I filled Tyler and John in on the facts I'd gleaned from Chief Kells. Tyler volunteered to write the news story. Fine with me since it allowed me to focus on my editorial and sped up the process of getting everything posted on our website. I told him to make sure to include the plea for witnesses. Then I sent Phil out to Echo Park to get whatever shots he could of the crime scene, assigned John to interview Torrey's widow if he could manage it (not much chance) and/or her sister and brother-in-law. Royce, normally a laid-back kid, seemed excited by the news and asked if there was anything he could do. I told him to check the files for correspondence expressing undue rage toward Martin Torrey, the only thing he was qualified to do. He had no experience at writing anything but sports, and little enough of that. He'd been on staff only a few months, a placeholder until I could find a suitable replacement. His writing was barely competent, he was unreliable in attending to assignments and meeting deadlines, and when Angela was in the office, he spent more time making moon eyes at her than he did working. No future in journalism at all.

"You think this will be the end of it, Mr. Lowenstein?" he asked. "The rapes, I mean."

"If Torrey was the rapist, yes," I said. "Mayor Delahunt thinks he was."

"But you don't agree?"

"I seldom agree with anything the mayor says or does. You know that if you read my editorials."

"Oh, sure I do. So you don't believe Torrey was guilty?"

"I didn't say that. For once I hope Delahunt is right."

I had the gist of my editorial worked out in my head, so it didn't take long for me to write it. Tyler finished at about the same time. I posted both pieces on the website, then e-mailed our online subscribers en masse to let them know the articles were up—the modern equivalent of a newspaper extra. When Phil came back with pics, I'd get those up, too. And anything John came up with.

My juices were still flowing hot, thanks as much to that pompous bastard Delahunt as to the murder. Taking on small-time, self-aggrandizing politicos like him—skewering all varieties of phonies, blowhards, self-promoters, bigots, and climate-change naysayers (he was one those, too)—is one of the great pleasures of owning and editing a small-town newspaper.

That was my goal from the time I came out of journalism school and went to work as a cub reporter on the *Portland Press Herald.* I'm a damn good newspaperman, if I do say so myself, but I tend to be stubborn and opinionated, I prefer doing things my own way, and I don't take orders well. Cut out to be my own boss, if anyone ever was.

The first paper I saved up enough to buy, a six-page weekly in a small Idaho farm town, cost me my marriage. Eleanor hated the town, the people, the long hours I put in, and eventually me. I wasn't sorry when she moved out and filed for divorce; I was glad of it because she didn't want custody of our seven-year-old kid and I did. I had to sell the sheet to pay Eleanor off, then go back to work as a wage slave to support Angela and me, but as things turned out, it was a small price to pay.

It took me nearly twelve years on three sheets, the last four on the *Sacramento Bee*, to save up enough to buy the *Clarion*. And at that, I couldn't have swung the deal if it weren't for a couple of friends willing to take a chance and put up enough cash to buy a one-third interest. So far their faith in me and mine in myself had paid off. The *Clarion* had been losing money when I took over; now it was finally in the black, if only just. An aggressive campaign had brought in more advertising revenue. That, and better news reportage, better features, and some judicious controversy had substantially increased our print and online subscription lists. The recent crime wave had been a factor, too. As much as I hated violence in general and violence against women in particular, sensationalism sold newspapers and always would.

Angela had also been an important part of the *Clarion*'s modest success. She had come up with the ad campaign, working in consort with the new advertising manager I hired, and also handled the bookkeeping duties. I was afraid she wouldn't be part of the team much longer, though. The newspaper business wasn't as vital to her as it was to me. What she had inherited was the same need to be her own boss. Once she finished the night business courses she was taking at Valley JC down in Riverton, her plan was to join a CPA firm and then eventually start one of her own. Here in Santa Rita, I hoped, but probably not if she married her current boyfriend. And that could happen. Tony Ciccoti was the only young man she'd ever been serious about, the one problem with him being that he was from Southern California and intended to move back there one day.

Angela and I had always had a kind of father-daughter psychic connection, and thinking about her sometimes triggered it. Did today. I was about to have a cup of coffee with Tyler when she called on my cell.

Every time I saw her or heard her voice on the phone the past few months, I felt a sense of relief that she was all right. She kept telling me not to worry about her, she was always careful and knew how to take care of herself, but I worried just the same. And would keep on worrying as long as she lived by herself. I loved that girl like crazy. She was all I had except for the *Clarion*.

"I just heard the news, Daddy. You're at the office, right?"

"Yep. Tyler's account and my editorial are finished and posted. Take a look, see what you think."

"I will, right away. Do the police have any leads yet?"

"No. Too soon."

She asked the same question Smith had, and that everybody else would soon be asking, and I gave her the same answer. Only time would tell. The important thing right now was the apprehension of Martin Torrey's assassin. Judging from the various people I'd spoken to and the general tone of the letters to the editor, the community continued to support Griff Kells and Robert Ortiz. But patience was running thin, and if the murder was not solved quickly, or if there were any more violent incidents to ratchet up public unrest, Delahunt and his city council cronies might succeed in throwing Kells to the wolves.

"Are you still coming to dinner tonight?" Angela asked.

Dinner tonight. At her apartment. I'd almost forgotten the invitation, hers and Tony Ciccoti's. He was evidently something of a gourmet cook—learned it from his father, who was a chef—and Angela was eager to show off his prowess. "I'll try to make it," I said. "Depends on whether or not anything else breaks between now and . . . what time, again?"

"Seven thirty. But we can make it later."

"I'll call you no later than six, so Tony won't have to cook too much food if I'm not there."

"He's Italian. He always cooks enough for four when there's just the two of us."

I sighed a little after we signed off. I'd miss her a lot if she married Ciccoti and moved away, especially if it was as far away as SoCal. Eleanor had been a bitch, and no more physically attractive than I was; how we'd managed to produce a sweet, beautiful, loyal, generous daughter like Angela was one of God's own miracles.

ROBERT ORTIZ

I WAS ANGRIER THAN I should have been at the murder of Martin Torrey. But I had wanted to prove that he was guilty of the serial assaults, arrest and charge him with the crimes, testify at his trial, see him convicted and sentenced to a long prison term—justice done according to the law. Now that he was dead, his guilt might never be proven. Even if there were no more rapes, the element of doubt would continue.

And now I would have to spend my time and energy hunting the person or persons responsible for his death. The irony in that was bitter.

The probable motive was revenge, carried out by an individual close to one of the assault victims or even by a victim herself. If this was true, then the list of possible suspects was fairly limited and solving the crime should be easier than tracking down an anonymous psychotic. In theory, anyway.

After Jack Spivey, the most likely candidate seemed to me to be Jason Palumbo, whose girlfriend, Courtney Reeves, was the most recent victim. Palumbo had not expressed extreme rage, as Spivey had, or made any veiled threats—it was his attitude and background that made me view him as capable of an impulsively foolish and violent act. Smart-mouthed, plainly contemptuous of the law, with a record of minor offenses: possession of marijuana and methamphetamine, possibly with intent to sell, though that had not been proven, and one count of mis-demeanor vandalism. As I had once said to Chief Kells, it was a short step from nonviolent to violent criminal behavior.

But a session with Palumbo would have to wait. He and the Reeves girl—her closest relative was an alcoholic mother—both worked days at the Riverfront Brew Pub on the river basin downtown, and I had no cause to brace him at his place of employment. Later today was soon enough, after I spoke with Spivey.

On the surface, the men closest to the other two victims, Neal Wilder and Arthur Pappas, were much less likely prospects. Wilder, husband of Sherry Wilder, was a successful architect, former one-term city councilman, and member of several civic organizations and the Santa Rita Country Club. Pappas, first cousin and only living relative of Eileen Jordan, was a produce manager at Safeway, a mild-mannered gay man whose contact with Miss Jordan was limited despite the fact that they lived only a few miles apart. Both men were law-abiding citizens, with not so much as a parking ticket to blemish their records, and neither owned a registered handgun. None of this completely ruled out either man, of course. They would be investigated along with everyone else who possessed a potential motive.

As to the victims, the only one who seemed capable of cold-blooded murder was Sherry Wilder. Very angry, very bitter. She had given no open indication of violent intent the times I had spoken to her, but her hatred of the man who had violated her was plainly more intense than that of any of the other women.

I made the Wilder home my next stop. It was in Rancho Estates, where many of the old, wealthy Santa Ritan Anglo families resided. Where Griff Kells and his wife also resided, though theirs was one of the smaller homes in the district. The Wilder house, perched high on the hillside above Echo Park, had been designed by Neal Wilder—a compact place of sharp edges, flat planes, and odd angles, constructed of redwood and a considerable amount of glass. It commanded a broad view of the river for half a mile in both directions, the fields and vineyards that stretched out to the distant hills on the opposite side of the valley. Wilder's vehicle, a new black Mercedes, was parked in the driveway.

I paused for a moment after I stepped from my cruiser, drawn by the view and a stirring of memory. Many years ago, not long after I began my career in law enforcement with the county sheriff's department, I had been one of the first officers on the scene of a brutal triple homicide in a migrant workers' camp across the river. A bracero named Jorge Martinez had gone berserk and slaughtered his wife and two children with a machete—the worst, the most sickening, crime scene of any I had witnessed before or since. Martinez had been seen fleeing through the vineyards, north along the river. In the manhunt that followed, as fortune would have it, I was the officer who discovered his hiding place. He still carried the bloody machete, but he made no threatening move toward me when I flushed him. Instead he again fled.

I pursued him in a fury, the images of his hacked-up wife and children like a fire in my mind. More than once I shouted for him to stop, but he did not, he stumbled toward the river in what I took to be a futile attempt at escape by swimming across it. It was then that I extended my sidearm and took running aim at his back.

Ley de fuga. The unwritten law of Latin American justice that empowers police to shoot fleeing fugitives with impunity, whether or not they are armed. Lynch law, vigilante justice.

I could have shot Martinez that day and gotten away with it. No other officer had been nearby, and at that time there was not as much antipolice sentiment or close scrutiny of the use of deadly force. But I did not give in to the fleeting urge. I am of Mexican lineage, but I do not believe in *ley de fuga* or any other such disregard for strict adherence to the laws of this country and the laws of God. I holstered my weapon, caught up to the terrified Martinez at the water's edge, and subdued him without violence. Later I received both a commendation and a promotion for my actions.

I do not condone vigilantism of any sort. Even if my wife or my daughters or some other member of my family were to be the victim of violence, God forbid, I would not take the law into my own hands. As much as the crime of rape disgusts and angers me, and as convinced as I am that Martin Torrey committed the four brutal assaults, I do not condone his murder, and I will do everything in my power to arrest without violence the person responsible as I arrested Jorge Martinez without violence that day across the river.

Neal Wilder opened the door to my ring—a distinguished-looking man of thirty-seven, with a precise mustache and thick dark hair silvering at the temples. He must have just returned from the country club, for his clothing was of the sort a man wears to play golf. He greeted me cordially and without surprise; news of Martin Torrey's assassination, as he put it, had reached him at the club, and he had driven straight home to share it with his wife.

"And your feelings about that, Mr. Wilder?"

"Mixed, I suppose. If Torrey was the rapist, I'm not sorry he's dead."

"Do you believe he was?"

"I don't know. With his past record, he could have been."

"You had no animosity toward him?"

"As matters stood, no. I would have, certainly, if he'd been proven guilty."

I asked if his wife was home, and when he said she was, I requested a few minutes of her time as well.

He seemed reluctant. "Is it necessary? That you talk to her, I mean."

"If you have no objection."

"Well, she's resting at the moment—"

"No, I'm not." Mrs. Wilder's voice, slightly thick, came from behind and to one side of him. "Don't just stand there, Neal. Invite the lieutenant in."

Her words made Wilder frown, a look quickly erased. He stepped aside, saying, "Yes, come in, Lieutenant," and cast a brief look at his wife, who was standing at the end of a hallway that led to the rear. After I was inside, Mrs. Wilder said, "Let's talk in the family room, shall we?" and turned immediately and a little unsteadily. A half-full glass in one hand explained the unsteadiness and the thickness in her voice. And her husband's reluctance.

I followed Wilder into a sunken room, the entire rear wall of which was floor-to-ceiling glass—windows and sliding doors. Beyond was a balcony that overlooked the higher hills to the east. Mrs. Wilder, a petite, ash blonde two years younger than her husband, had gone straight to a leather-and-chrome wet bar and was refilling her glass. The external wounds from the beating she'd received were no longer visible. I did not know if she'd been a heavy drinker before the assault or if her ordeal had led her to seek comfort in alcohol.

"We were having cocktails," she said. "I'd ask you to join us, Lieutenant, but I don't suppose you're allowed to drink on duty."

"No."

Neal Wilder invited me to sit down. I declined, saying, "I have only a few questions."

"About the Torrey homicide," he said. "Routine, I trust?"

"Yes."

"He wants to know where you were last night, darling," Mrs. Wilder said. "Shall I tell him?"

Wilder's frown reappeared. Without looking at her he said to me, "I was working late at my office on an important new design."

"For what period of time?"

"From late afternoon until after ten."

"The entire time? You had no dinner?"

"No. A late lunch, so I wasn't hungry."

"Was anyone with you?"

"No."

Mrs. Wilder made a sound that might have been a chuckle and drank deeply from her glass.

"Did you make or receive any phone calls?"

"No. No interruptions of any kind. Just steady work on the design." Then, after a short pause: "I suppose you're talking with everyone who might have had a reason to shoot Martin Torrey."

"Yes."

"Well, you can cross me off the list. I'm many things, Lord knows, but vengeful and crazy aren't among them."

"That's right," Mrs. Wilder said. "My dear husband is many things. Lord knows."

"Do you own a handgun?" I asked him.

"Absolutely not. I don't like guns, won't have one in the house. In fact I'm an active supporter of gun control. Sherry can tell you that."

"Oh, yes. Neal abhors all forms of violence. He's a lover, not a fighter."

"Were you home last evening, Mrs. Wilder?" I asked.

"Me? Don't tell me I'm under suspicion, too?"

"Please answer the question. *Were* you home the entire evening?"

"Yes, I was. But I can't prove it. No visitors, no calls. Just me all alone in this big empty house, waiting faithfully for Neal to come back from his . . . designs."

Wilder said through tightened lips, "Are we about through here now, Lieutenant?"

"One more question. Do either of you know of threats made by anyone against Martin Torrey's life?"

"I don't," he said. "People I know believed him guilty, but threats . . . no."

Mrs. Wilder shook her head. "Do *you* think he was guilty?" she asked me.

"There was insufficient evidence to charge him with the crimes."

"Which means you did and still do. If I knew it for sure, I'd dance on his grave."

"But you wouldn't have killed him."

"I don't know, maybe I would. But I didn't." She laughed suddenly, the kind of hiccuping laugh fueled by liquor. "Wienie-wagger in Ohio, rapist in California. *Wienie-wagger.* That's what you call men who expose themselves in public, isn't it?"

"It is a term for it, yes."

"What do you call a man who grabs a woman in a public park and does a hell of a lot more than just wag his wienie at her? Wienie-stuffer? Wienie-stabber? Wienie-buggerer?"

"Sherry, for God's sake . . ."

"Never mind." She emptied her glass in a long convulsive swallow. "It doesn't matter as long as he was the one and now he's dead. Him and his goddamn wienie."

Wilder went with me to the front door. "I'm sorry for my wife's behavior," he said in an undertone. "She hasn't been the same since it happened. The trauma . . . you understand."

"I understand."

Before driving away, I sat for a few seconds looking up at the house, going over the interrogations in my mind. I did not think Neal Wilder was the person we were after. But I was not so sure about his wife.

SHERRY WILDER

I WAS ABOUT TO pour myself another scotch when Neal came back into the living room and said, "Did you have to be so nasty while Ortiz was here? God knows what he thinks of us."

"I don't care what he thinks of us."

"Or what I think either, apparently."

"Very perceptive of you, darling."

He sighed as I filled my glass. "Do you really need another drink?"

"Yes, I really need it."

"It's not even four o'clock. The way you're going, you'll pass out before dinner."

"All the better for you if I do. Then you won't have to make an excuse to slip out and go see your girlfriend."

"Oh, God, please don't start that again—"

"Afraid I was going to tell Ortiz that's where you really were last night, weren't you?"

"I was working on a design, just as I told him and you—"

"Working on Gloria Ryder is more like it. Is she a good fuck?"

He sighed again and gave me one of his weary, long-suffering looks. "How many times do I have to say it? I am not having an affair with Gloria or any other woman."

"That's what you swore five years ago. What was her name? Let's see . . . Donna? No, Donelle."

"All right. I made a mistake—a one-weekend mistake, that's all. It's the only time I've been unfaithful to you."

"Until after the rape anyhow."

"The only time, period."

"Even though I haven't let you come near me since?"

"Yes."

"Bullshit. You're too virile, Neal   you couldn't go without sex for four weeks, let alone four months."

"Well, I have. And I'll continue to until you're ready."

"Ready. My God, ready! To be your sperm receptacle again."

He actually winced. "That's unfair, Sherry."

"Ah, but accurate."

"No, it's not. Have I asked you even once to start making love again?"

"No need, when you've got Gloria."

"Damn it, I don't have or want any woman but you! Why can't you believe that?" Then, when I drank instead of answering him: "You're so different, so . . . changed. If only you hadn't gone jogging that night—"

"Oh, so now I'm to blame? Stupid Sherry, jogging in the park after dark like she did a hundred times before, just begging to be raped."

"I didn't mean it that way. I'm not the enemy, for Christ's sake. I understand how you feel, how much you've suffered—"

"Do you really?" The scar on my neck throbbed; I reached up under the hair I'd let grow long to cover it, not that rubbing helped any. The shrink I'd seen for a time said that scar tissue was dead tissue and what I was feeling was phantom pain. So what? The goddamn thing *hurt*. Was I supposed to feel better knowing the pain wasn't real? "Have you ever been beaten up, sliced by a knife, had some stranger's wienie slammed into your ass? You don't understand a thing."

"I try. I've been there for you the past four months, in every way that matters. I give you as much support as I know how. But all you do is reject me, accuse me of things that aren't true when you talk to me at all. It's as if—"

"As if what?"

"You've started hating me. And not just me—all men because of what one sick bastard did to you."

Man-hater? No, I didn't think so. Well, maybe, to a certain extent. My new friend the Pink Lady indicated a tendency in that direction, didn't she? I'd have to think about it some more. Neal watched me drain my glass in that pained way of his. "And I drink too much now, too," I said, "don't forget that."

"Yes, you do."

"You never used to think I drank too much. You used to like me to drink because it made me horny."

"I never encouraged you to drink nonstop, all day, every day, until you pass out."

"Did it ever occur to you that that's the only way I can sleep?"

"Yes, but it's not a healthy sleep. And not the kind of crutch you can lean on for very long—"

"So you think I've become an alcoholic."

"You'll end up one if you don't exercise some control."

"Maybe I should join AA. 'Hello, my name is Sherry, and my husband says I'm a drunk.'"

"If you'd just try therapy again, individually or group—"

"Therapy! Two miserable months of strangers poking and prodding at me like an animal in a cage, making me relive that night over and over until I was ready to scream. No. No more of that. Johnnie Walker here is all the therapy I need."

Neal made a noise and threw up his hands like an exasperated little boy. "There's no use trying to talk to you when you're like this. I'm going to take a shower."

"Good idea. Get all nice and clean and put on some of that Versace cologne of yours. Gloria loves it, I'll bet."

He started across the room. When he was almost to the steps leading up to the bedrooms, I stopped him by saying, "Neal." And then: "Do you want a divorce?"

"What? No, of course not."

"Are you sure?"

"I'm sure. As difficult as things are right now, no, I do not want a divorce."

He went away and I went back to the wet bar. "I think," I said to Johnnie Walker, "I think maybe I do."

GRIFFIN KELLS

FRANK JUDKINS AND I were just winding up a not-very-productive conference when the report came in that Martin Torrey's five-year-old Camry had been located. Judkins was a year shy of sixty now, with thirty-five years on the force—a heavyset, plodding man, his bald, ovoid head covered with liver spots like a speckled egg. None too bright, in my estimation, his rise to the captaincy based more on politics than merit. We were civil with each other, but there was no love lost between us. Like Mayor Delahunt, he thought he should have been promoted to chief instead of the city council's hiring an outsider with twenty years' less experience.

Patrol officers Chang and Gonsolves had spotted the Camry on South Street, a side street in the industrial area between the river and the railroad yards. The doors were all locked; they'd opened the driver's door with a widow bar to get a closer look at the interior and to trip the trunk release. Their cursory examination revealed nothing of importance. Seats and floorboards empty, the trunk bare except for a spare tire, a blanket, a first-aid kit. No visible bloodstains or other signs of violence.

While Judkins went to send Joe Bloom down there for a complete evidence check, I contacted Robert Ortiz. He had nothing to report so far, other than Jack Spivey's apparent alibi for the time of the shooting. He said he'd join Bloom for the inspection of Torrey's vehicle.

South Street. The location deepened the mystery surrounding last night's events. Had Torrey gone there to meet someone? Had he then been forced to leave the Camry in that location? Or had the perp later abandoned it there for some reason? If that last was the answer, a spare key had to have been used since Torrey's key had been on the ring in his coat pocket. All three possibilities indicated abduction, though it was conceivable that Torrey had willingly accompanied his killer. In which case the perp had to have been known to him and an acceptable pretext given for the crosstown ride to Echo Park.

But why the park, miles away from South Street? The industrial area was even more deserted on Friday nights after dark. Why not just shoot Torrey and let his body be discovered right there?

Too damn many questions. And with the motive still in question, and assuming Spivey's alibi held up, too many potential suspects.

Another possibility had to be considered, too—that Torrey had been killed for a reason unrelated to the criminal assaults, and that the perp had fired those groin shots, then arranged the body as he had, to make it look like a revenge or vigilante killing. Robert and I had discussed that, and he was inclined to dismiss it—given his stubborn certainty that Torrey had committed the rapes—but I was keeping an open mind.

So little to go on at this early stage. The contents of Torrey's pockets had yielded nothing but the usual items men carry: key ring, inexpensive pocketknife, quarter and two dimes, a wallet containing fourteen dollars, a fairly old photograph of Liane Torrey, and not much else. No cell phone; Torrey had had one, so if it wasn't in the Camry, then the perp must have taken it away with him. I didn't expect the autopsy report, when it finally came in, to tell us anything; cause of death was all too obvious. There was a slim chance a forensic examination of the deceased's clothing would turn up some trace evidence—strands of hair, traceable fibers or powders or soil particles—but I wouldn't have wanted to bet on it.

Another long shot: a witness or witnesses to whatever had gone down at South Street who would voluntarily come forward. Still, long shots do come in once in a while. I put in a call to the *Clarion* office, told Ted Lowenstein of the discovery of the Camry, asked him to include that information in his Internet postings. He didn't have anything for me—no notably inflammatory correspondence from any reader that was worth following up on.

I swiveled around to my computer, pulled up the new file on the homicide. Joe Bloom had uploaded the photos he'd taken at the crime scene; I slow-scanned through them. The close-ups of the victim and the immediate area around him were clear and sharp. The position of the body had raised questions in my mind at the scene and did so again now.

A revenge or vigilante killing inferred a combination of rage and hate, coldly controlled because of the apparent premeditation. The point-blank round to the head was consistent with that, as were the two bullets in the groin. What wasn't consistent was the crucified position. Why lay Torrey out like that after killing him? It must have been done that way on purpose. Patrolman Malatesta's theory that Torrey had been shot in the groin first to make him suffer didn't fit the facts; a man mutilated in such a fashion would have thrashed around in agony, dug the heels of his shoes into the grass, clawed up clumps of it. Bloom's photos, and the emptiness of the victim's hands and lack of grass residue under his fingernails, proved none of that had taken place. Execution first, mutilation second.

So why the postmortem arrangement of the body? Robert and I had discussed that at the scene, too, and the only theory that seemed to make any sense was twisted religious symbolism. Kill an allegedly evil man, then stretch him out like the good man who had died for our sins two millennia ago. If that was the answer, then it followed that the perp had strong religious leanings. Which if true made the job of identifying him that much more difficult. It's only the flagrant zealots who advertise their beliefs.

I clicked through the other crime-scene photos. The only one that showed anything definite was a round indentation in the grass near the corpse's head, where the perp had knelt to fire the head shot. It seemed fairly large and deep, man-size, but it *could* have been made by a woman. Inconclusive. And useless as evidence unless whatever garment had been worn over the knee could be found unwashed and any soil and grass stains examined—a highly improbable prospect.

COURTNEY REEVES

THE FIRST THING JASON did after Lieutenant Ortiz left was to go get a couple of joints from his stash. He offered me one, but I shook my head. I used to like smoking dope with him, but ever since the night I was raped, it doesn't get me high or mellow anymore, just kind of paranoid.

He lit one and took a long hit off it. "Man, that's good shit. Pure gold. Sure you don't want some?"

"I'm sure," I said. "It's a good thing you weren't smoking before Ortiz showed up."

"Yeah. That Mexican cop's got it in for me. He's just looking for an excuse to bust my ass."

"We shouldn't have lied to him, Jason."

"The hell we shouldn't. What was I supposed to do, tell him I was out buying half a key of Jamaican weed last night?"

"You were gone a long time . . ."

"So? I told you, Russ was late for our meet and then afterwards we smoked a couple and had a few beers together." Jason frowned at me through the smoke. "You're not getting ideas in your head, are you?"

Well, I was. A few. I couldn't help it. He said he'd been out with Russ, but what if it was Pooch? Pooch was a bad dude. He cooked and sold meth and he'd gotten Jason started on it right after me and him hooked up, not just using but selling, too. Jason had been kind of screwed up when he was on meth, but he'd quit after he got busted for possession and promised me he'd never have anything more to do with the stuff or with Pooch. But I couldn't help being afraid he was hanging out with that fat weirdo again. I wanted to ask him about it but I was scared to. So I didn't.

"No," I said. "It's just . . . What if the cop finds out? That we weren't home together all evening, I mean."

"How's he gonna find out if we stick to the story?"

"I don't know. I'm just worried, that's all."

"Well, don't be. He won't find out about the dope and he won't pin what happened to that Torrey dude on me, either. No way."

"You really think he was the rapist? Torrey?"

"Sure he was. Sure. He was there in the Riverfront when you blabbed about walking the dog, wasn't he?"

"I didn't blab, it just slipped out while I was talking to Mrs. Lyman."

"Whatever. He was there, that's the point, so he knew right where to wait for you. It had to be him."

"I guess so. I hope so."

Ladybug started whining again in the kitchen. I'd put her out there when Lieutenant Ortiz showed up. She's real friendly and I didn't want her jumping all over him like she did the first time he came to the apartment. I went out there and got her. My wrist is mostly healed, but I still have to be careful picking her up even though she doesn't weigh very much. I had to be real careful at Riverfront, too, now that the cast was off and I was back at work, not to carry glasses and trays the way I used to.

I don't know what breed Ladybug is. I got her from the animal shelter and they didn't know either, but she's got this soft fur that's a sort of orangey brown with little black spots here and there like one of those cute little ladybugs. She wiggled against me on the couch like she does, wagging her tail and licking my chin.

Jason made a face. "Stupid dog."

"She's not stupid, she's a sweetie. Aren't you, Ladybug?"

"What good is she? Didn't even try to protect you that night, just turned tail and ran."

"She's only a little dog."

"Came home and hid in the bushes out front. Not a peep out of her. If she'd barked, I would've gone out and found you a lot sooner."

"It's not her fault. She hardly ever barks—you always said that was what you liked about her, how quiet she is."

"Yeah, well . . ."

Neither of us said anything for a while after that. Jason finished his first joint and fired up the second and smoked that one pretty fast. *Uh-oh,* I thought then. He had that look on his face, like he did sometimes when he was high.

"How about we go to bed?" he said.

"It's too early for bed—"

"Not too early for what I'm thinking about."

"Honey, I can't yet. I just . . . can't."

"It's been five weeks now. You're all healed up. Besides, I just want to do it the usual way."

Outside I was healed up, but not inside. I still got bad headaches, and pain sometimes when I went to the toilet. Just the thought of sex made me go all cold and twitchy. "I want to, honest I do," I said, "but I'm not ready yet."

"Yeah. Right. But five weeks is a long time for a guy to go without. You could give me head. Or a hand job at least."

"I can't do that, either. I wish I could, for you, but I *can't*. Please don't be mad at me. Please."

"I'm not mad at you."

Oh, God, I thought for about the dozenth time, *what if I'm never ready for sex again? What if what happened that night made me frigid? Jason's such a stud, he can't get enough . . . What if he leaves me because I can't make him happy in bed anymore?*

My eyes were wet, all of a sudden. A sob built up in my throat. I held on tight to Ladybug and buried my face in her fur.

"Hey, you crying?"

"No . . . no . . ."

"Yeah, you are." He got up from his chair and came over to the couch and sat down next to me, pushing Ladybug away so he could put his arm around me. "Hey, come on, there's nothing to cry about."

"I'm so sorry, Jason . . ."

"Hey, it's not your fault. I know how hard it's been for you. Every time I think about what that son of a bitch did to you . . ." He shook his head, pulled mine in against his chest. "It's over now," he said then. "Won't be long before everything's back to the way it used to be. Right?"

"God, I hope so. I love you, Jason."

"I know it."

"You still love me, don't you?"

"Sure I do. Sure."

We sat quiet for a time. Then he said, "Let's get something to eat. I'm starving."

Weed always made him hungry as well as horny. I wasn't. I didn't have much appetite; I'd lost four pounds from not eating since it happened. But I said, "I'll go fix us something."

"No, you won't. I feel like going out. Celebrating with a pizza and a pitcher of beer."

"Celebrating what?"

He winked at me. "What do you think?"

EILEEN JORDAN

ARTHUR CALLED TO TELL me the news about Martin Torrey. He was excited, or as excited as he ever becomes, but I had no reaction. Whether Torrey was the invader or not was of little importance. I didn't tell Arthur that. It would only have dismayed him.

"I would've come and told you in person," he said, "but . . . well . . ."

"You needn't explain."

He cleared his throat. "How are you feeling?"

"Well enough," I lied.

"No, um, complications or anything?"

"No."

"That's a relief. How soon are you going to start teaching again?"

"I don't know."

"Eileen, are you sure you're all right? You sound . . . I don't know, listless, distant."

"Do I? I don't feel that way," I lied.

"But you don't seem very . . ." He cleared his throat again. "Well, I thought the news would perk you up."

"Why should a man's violent death perk me up?"

"If he was the one who attacked you . . ."

"Do the police know now that he was?"

"No, I don't think so. But whoever killed him believed it."

"I don't condone murder, Arthur. Not for any reason."

There was a small silence. "Well . . . George and I just wanted you to know in case you hadn't heard."

No, George hadn't. George Medlock was the reason Arthur had telephoned instead of coming in person. George disliked me as much as I disliked him, a mutual distaste that had nothing to do with his and Arthur's sexual orientation. I have no prejudice against homosexuals. I do have a prejudice against bullies and lazy individuals who refuse to seek gainful employment. Arthur paid all their bills and was rewarded with abuse—verbal, and for all I knew physical.

"Thank you," I said. "I appreciate the call."

"If there's anything you need . . ." He'd said that before, half a dozen times.

"Yes, I'll let you know. Good-bye, Arthur."

I had been dozing in Grandmother's slat-backed walnut rocker when he called. My nights had been mostly sleepless since the invasion. That was how I thought of it, an invasion not only of my body but of my life, my soul. Until that night I had been unafraid of the dark; now I kept it at bay with lamplight from dusk until dawn. And still I couldn't sleep. Night sounds refused to allow it; no matter how ordinary, they seemed like little whispers of menace. Brief naps during the day had become a necessity.

The tea I had brewed earlier was cold. Brew another pot? It didn't seem worth the effort. I lowered myself slowly and carefully onto the thick cushion I had placed on the chair. At my age broken bones and internal injuries do not heal as rapidly as they once would have. Even after almost two months, every movement I made caused considerable discomfort.

I sat listening to the empty silence. I had lived in this tiny cottage for nineteen years now, ever since moving from Walnut Creek to accept the teaching position at South Santa Rita Elementary School. Three rooms and a bathroom just large enough for a stall shower. Tiny front yard, somewhat larger backyard and garden. No garage or carport. The rent was reasonable enough, though the owner had seen fit to raise it again last year.

Home. For the rest of my days. The only real home Miss (never Ms.) Eileen Jordan had ever had.

I looked around the oh-so-familiar living room. Wall of books, mostly classics acquired at thrift shops and library sales, small credenza, small love seat (a misnomer here if ever there was one), cretonne-covered armchair, elderly television set, roller cart on one side of the rocker that served as an end table, floor lamp on the other side. And in the other rooms, utilitarian basics—and a full-length bedroom mirror that I had turned to the wall after my return home from the hospital.

How long had it been since my last visitor? The better part of a week. At first I had a sporadic stream of them, mostly during my four-day stay in the hospital. The police, of course. Arthur. Barbara Jacobs, my one and only real friend. Nancy Potter, a casual acquaintance. Principal Tate and three fellow teachers at South Santa Rita Elementary. None had stayed longer than a few minutes, and all except Susan Sinclair, the victims' advocate, had seemed uncomfortable as well as sympathetic. Only the policewoman, Barbara, and Mrs. Bellarmine from across the street had come to the house during the early period of convalescence. And only Barbara more than once, to bring me groceries and medicines until I was well enough to go out on my own, though she still called every two or three days to ask how I was.

Alone again now, as I had been most of my life. An unattractive, middle-aged old-maid schoolteacher—a literal stereotype—with no surviving relatives except Arthur, no close confidantes, not even a pet because the owner refused to allow so much as a caged parakeet. Unwanted and unloved. Teaching not because it fulfilled me as it once had, but because I had no other skills and no other prospects. Neither a popular nor an unpopular teacher, neither a good nor a bad one. Half a century on this earth, and I had done nothing worthwhile, nothing that made a difference in anyone's life. Not one of my former students had ever sought me out to say that I had been a motivating force in even the smallest of ways. Not one in thirty years.

Once I had consoled myself with the thought that my life would have been different if David had not been killed in the Persian Gulf. David, the only man I ever cared for who had shown interest in me in return. David, the only man I had ever willingly allowed inside my body—on two occasions before he was shipped overseas, and so long ago I could barely remember the experience. But over the years I had grown less and less convinced that he would have kept his promise of marriage if he had survived the war. More likely he would have found someone else, someone more attractive than a tall, spare woman with the kind of face a cruel individual had once likened to a horse's, and breasts another cruel individual had referred to as being "like two fried eggs."

Portrait of a barren life.

I made an effort to banish these bleak musings, without success. Before the invasion, I hadn't often permitted an indulgence in self-pity; I had wrapped myself in an insulating blanket of normalcy. Now I seemed incapable of pretense any longer. Nothing cheered me. Not the prospect of returning to my classroom duties, or I would have done so by now. Not gardening—I hadn't tended to the plants in the backyard since coming home. Not reading—my powers of concentration were no longer acute. Not the classical music of Brahms and Beethoven I had once enjoyed—it all seemed overly loud now, bombastic. Now and then I would turn on the television, but for the sound of voices rather than for knowledge or diversion.

It was as if I had been infected by a debilitating disease that had no cure. That was why the sudden demise of the man who may have been responsible had no effect on me. It made no difference who the invader was. The invasion itself was all that mattered. The act had ravaged me and would continue to ravage me for as long as I lived.

GRIFFIN KELLS

Martin Torrey's abandoned vehicle had contained no useful evidence. Joe and Robert had gone over it carefully before having it towed to the police impound garage for further examination. The glove compartment contained the usual insurance and registration papers and little else. Nothing was hidden under the seats, the floor mats, or the interior or trunk carpeting. Perhaps Joe would find something when he fingerprinted and vacuumed the interior, but none of us held out much hope of it.

I pulled up the combined files on the four rapes. I'd combed through them a dozen times before and I knew each by heart, but now that our primary suspect was dead, another look couldn't hurt.

There was no doubt that the assaults had all been committed by the same man; his actions and what vague piecemeal descriptions we'd gathered from the victims proved that. Average size and weight, of indeterminate age, and strong. Wore a ski mask, gloves, dark clothing. Wielded a knife of unknown type, threatened to cut the victims' throats if they resisted. Forced each to lie facedown, ripped off clothing and underpants while spewing threats and obscenities in a raspy voice, then brutally beat and sodomized them. The attacks had been increasingly violent. Robert was of the opinion that if they were to continue, the next victim might not survive. I agreed with him.

Whoever the serial was, he'd been cunning and incredibly lucky. Four assaults in four months despite increased police patrols, stepped-up neighborhood watches, public warnings to women not to go out alone at night and to take security precautions when home by themselves. And each one committed without leaving a single solid clue to his identity.

No DNA evidence. A condom had been used each time and carried away afterward, none of the victims had managed to mark the man in any way, and no hairs or saliva or any other testable substance had been discovered. Sexual-assault evidence kits had been assembled on three of the four victims—Eileen Jordan had refused, her prerogative—and the only one processed so far, from the first victim, Sherry Wilder, had yielded nothing of any use. Chances were the two on-hold kits wouldn't either, when they were finally processed.

No crime-scene evidence of any consequence. No significant mouth or body odors other than a general agreement among the victims that the assailant was clean smelling, as if he'd washed or showered not long before. No witnesses to anyone lurking in the areas before or after the assaults. And no significant pattern to his MO other than the use of a knife, the sodomizing and battering of the victims, the foul language, and threats of bodily harm. Usually in serial cases there are similarities in the places and types of victim chosen. Not so in this one. The crimes had taken place in different sections of town, on different nights of the week. The victims were of different ages, body types, hair color, employment, and social status. None knew or had any connection with the others, except for the tenuous and indirect link that had put Robert onto Martin Torrey in the first place.

Sherry Wilder. Age twenty-five. Married, no children. Slender, athletic. Blonde. Residence: Rancho Estates. Part-time instructor at Norden's Health & Fitness downtown. Date of assault: December 16, last year. Place and time: Echo Park, approximately seven P.M. She often went jogging in the park, usually during daylight hours, but on that day chose the evening because of a late stay at the fitness club and the unseasonably warm weather. Attacked and dragged off one of the paths into the woods northeast of the children's playground. She fought him, despite the knife, and he gashed her neck above the shoulder, a deep four-inch wound that required stitches.

Ione Spivey. Age forty. Married, one child. Stocky. Brunette. Housewife. Residence: Denton Street, a lower-middle-class neighborhood. Date of assault: January 19. Place and time: her home, approximately nine P.M. Alone in the house, her husband away on an overnight delivery to the Bay Area, her son spending the night with a friend. Home-invasion assault, entrance gained through an unlocked kitchen door. She had just gotten out of the bathtub and was entering the bedroom when the light suddenly went out and she was grabbed and dragged to the bed. Punched in the face when she screamed, the blow breaking her nose. Punched again and her cheek cut when she attempted to open the night-stand drawer where her husband kept his .38 revolver. Submitted passively after that. Perp took the handgun with him when he left, the only time he'd stolen anything from his victims.

Eileen Jordan. Age fifty. Unmarried. Tall, thin. Gray haired. Schoolteacher, fourth and fifth grades at South Santa Rita Elementary. Residence: Pine Court, middle-class neighborhood, southeast side. Date of assault: February 15. Place and time: South Santa Rita Elementary, seven forty-five P.M. She'd driven to the school to retrieve some forgotten notes for a lesson she was preparing. Grabbed from behind while on her way to her classroom from the parking lot at the rear and assaulted in a grassy area between two wings. Despite passive submission, battered repeatedly on the head, neck, and rib cage during the act, resulting in two broken ribs. Also suffered severe rectal damage.

Courtney Reeves. Age twenty-two. Petite. Ash-blonde hair, turquoise streaked in the modern fashion. Unmarried. Employed as a waitress at the Riverfront Brew Pub, where her live-in boyfriend, Jason Palumbo, also worked as a bartender. Residence: apartment at 2644 Ninth Street, across from the high school football and track field. Date of assault: March 9. Place and time: under the west-side bleachers, approximately eight P.M. Accosted while on her way home from walking her dog on the field, the side gate to which had at that time been left unsecured at night. Struck violently on the head when she struggled and cried out, then thrown to the ground with enough force to break her right wrist. The dog had been of no help to her, having fled as soon as she was accosted. In addition to the broken wrist, suffered a concussion and multiple cuts, contusions, and abrasions.

Rape is about power, not sex, and is usually though not always motivated by a pathological hatred of women. Whoever had committed these atrocities was a sicker, more sadistic predator than most. A psycho who needed to satisfy his demons monthly, who would eventually cross the line into homicide if he wasn't stopped. All the more reason to hope Robert was right and he'd already been stopped.

We'd painstakingly interviewed dozens of individuals. Santa Rita had eight registered sex offenders, none with a record of violent rape, all with unbreakable alibis for one or more of the assaults. Same with registered sex offenders in this county and neighboring counties. Same with men who had records of domestic violence or crimes against women involving actual or threatened physical abuse. Not a single viable suspect had surfaced until the fourth assault, when the link that led Robert to suspect Martin Torrey had turned up.

Robert had spoken to Torrey at Soderholm Brewery after the assault on Ione Spivey, one of a half dozen warehouse employees who knew in advance that her husband would be away from home on an overnight haul. Torrey's name came up again when Courtney Reeves gave her statement. Few people knew that she walked her dog alone on the football field at night, she said; she didn't advertise that because dogs were prohibited on school grounds. But she remembered revealing her "secret" during a conversation about dogs and dog-walking with one of the brew pub's women customers. One other person had been within earshot at the time—the man delivering kegs of Soderholm beer, Martin Torrey.

A tenuous link at best, and to only two of the assaults, but enough to tweak Robert's bloodhound instincts. Torrey had been nervous, somewhat evasive, during a second round of questioning. That, plus his inability to supply alibis for the times of any of the assaults (the claimed penchant for solitary night driving), his average size and the strength necessary to wrestle kegs and cases of beer, and that he was a loner not particularly well liked by the brewery's other employees, had raised the red flag even higher. An NICS background check had revealed Torrey's past history in Ohio, and that in turn led to the discovery of his failure to register as a sex offender with the California justice system.

His case history and psychological profiles, which we'd received from the Ohio authorities, showed him to be what was termed a paraphiliac, his voyeuristic urges dating back to his midteens. It wasn't the sight of naked women that got him excited, it was the secrecy in spying on them. He hadn't approached any of his three peeping victims, only fantasized about having sex with them while masturbating. According to the psychiatrist who'd examined him prior to his trial, and to the ones who'd treated him after he was institutionalized, he harbored no aggressive tendencies toward women and was a danger only to himself. They stated that he was deeply ashamed of his affliction and consumed with self-hatred, but he had responded well to therapy and been pronounced fit to return to society after nine months.

The caveat in all of this, a consulting psychiatrist in Sacramento had told me, was that paraphilia had no cure and could not only reoccur but in rare cases mutate into other, dangerous forms of sexual perversion. Among the causes in those cases were frustrations in the individual's day-to-day existence, changes in his attitudes and feelings toward women, the inability to derive satisfaction from normal sexual relations, and the viewing of violent forms of pornography.

This information plus the felony failure-to-register charge was enough, once we had Torrey in custody, for a judge to grant search warrants for his home and the Camry. But we hadn't found even one scrap of evidence linking him to the assaults. Nor had we found any printed or computerized pornography in his possession. He'd vehemently denied any interest in porn, and both he and his wife refused to discuss their sex life.

Ted Lowenstein had played down the investigation and the felony-arrest story in the *Clarion*, but the county's largest newspaper, the *Riverton Sentinel*, gave it plenty of space and also ran a photograph of Torrey. One of the TV stations did likewise. His wife's scraping together enough money to meet his bail kept him in the public eye, his freedom fuel for fear, anger, resentment.

And so here we were, once more in a holding pattern exacerbated now by Torrey's assassination. Was he or wasn't he the serial? If he was, how were we going to prove it? If he wasn't, how were we going to catch a mystery man, who had eluded us for four months, before he struck again?

There was a knock on the door and Sergeant Eversham poked his head inside. "First out-of-town reporters just showed up, clamoring for an interview with you. Send them in or stall them?"

I stifled a sigh. "No point in stalling. Go ahead, send them in."

ROBERT ORTIZ

I MADE MY SECOND visit to the Spivey home after determining that Jack Spivey had returned from his hunting trip with his son. Although I was careful not to say anything to him that could be taken as an accusation, he was upset at being questioned and surly as a result. He admitted threatening Martin Torrey in the Safeway parking lot—"I couldn't stand to see him walking around loose after what he done, I just lost it for a minute, that's all. I never would've shot the son of a bitch, but I'm glad somebody did. You find the guy blew him away, I'll shake his hand." But Spivey's alibi appeared solid. He had gone bowling on Friday evening, as Mrs. Spivey had told me, and he provided the names of teammates on the Soderholm Strikers as witnesses to the fact.

Jason Palumbo remained a suspect despite his and Courtney Reeves's claim that he had not left their apartment Friday night. One spouse or partner will often lie to protect the other. And I still did not care for Palumbo's smug attitude, his approval of the manner of Martin Torrey's death. My gut instinct was that he was capable of homicidal revenge, particularly if he was under the influence of drugs. The only doubt I had concerned his ability to premeditate a crime with as many oddities and complexities as this one appeared to have.

Sherry Wilder was the only other suspect thus far. Her alibi was insupportable, her anger and hatred were very much on the surface, and she appeared to have developed an alcohol problem. Liquor mixed with rage can be a lethal combination.

It was nearly seven when I left the Spivey home. I checked in with Griff again—he was still in his office, as I expected he would be. He'd put in many long hours since the serial rapes began and would continue to do so until that case and the Martin Torrey homicide were resolved. Captain Judkins, had he been promoted to chief, would not have been up to the task. *No le pidas peras al olmo.* An old Mexican proverb that translates to "Do not ask something from someone who cannot do the job."

I did not envy Griff's position in the slightest. I have no difficulty commanding men, but no aptitude for administrative duties and little for public relations, and I do not suffer fools well; I would not make a proper police chief in Santa Rita or anywhere else. My goal is to become a high-ranking detective with the state police or the police department of one of the larger cities. Such a place in law enforcement best suits my abilities. I had not yet applied for one because Sofia and I did not want to uproot our family while our daughters were still in school, but perhaps one would be forthcoming if I was instrumental in ending the crime wave here. One can always hope.

In my father's time, rising even to the rank of detective lieutenant in a town the size of Santa Rita would have been difficult if not impossible for a Mexican American. Now, with Hispanics comprising more than 40 percent of California's population, professional and political opportunities for men and women of my race have risen substantially. Not to an unlimited degree, nor will they as long as racism has a voice, but perhaps when any grandchildren Sofia and I are blessed with are grown, that day of unlimited opportunity will come. After all, who would have thought as recently as twenty years ago that a half-black man would be elected president?

There was no need for me to return to the station tonight. I drove home to Riverview Acres, the new subdivision in the low hills east of town where we had lived for five years. The house and property are of good size, attractive enough in the modern ranch style, comfortable enough, but not the sort of permanent home I wished my family to have.

If there was to be a larger, more attractive, more comfortable one for us, it would not be in this town where I had lived most of my life.

Sofia met me with words of comfort. A beautiful woman inside and out, my Sofia. I marveled to look at her, for she might still be the girl of twenty I had married eighteen years ago. Her face, Madonna-like to my eye, was unlined, and not a single strand of gray blemished her thick black hair. No day passed that I did not thank God for uniting us.

I kissed her, held her in a tight embrace. Yet I did not take as much simple pleasure in the moment as I would have at another time. Behind her I could see the large bronze crucifix adorning our living room wall, and once again I thought of the strangeness of the pose of Martin Torrey's body. Why had his killer laid him out in such a blasphemous way? Mocking religious symbolism, as Griff had suggested? A twisted apology to God for having broken the fifth commandment? The contrary offering of a damned soul to Satan? Or was there another reason for the unholy pose, sane or insane, that might be a clue to the perp's identity?

Sofia was speaking to me. "You must be hungry, *querido*."

I wasn't, but I said, "Yes. A little."

"Come into the kitchen. I'll fix you something."

"Where are the girls?" I asked, following her.

"Daniela's in her room, no doubt talking or texting on her phone."

"What a surprise." The girl, fourteen now, might as well have had the instrument surgically attached to her hand, if not her ear; she was never without it, even while she slept, she kept it under her pillow. "Valentina? In her room as well?"

"No. Out on a date."

"A date?"

"It's Saturday night."

"Not with that Rodriguez kid. I don't trust him—"

"No. She has a new boyfriend. Joe O'Reilly."

"O'Reilly. An Anglo."

"Irish. But his people aren't supporters of the IRA."

"Please, Sofia, I'm not in the mood for jokes. What do you know about him?

"He's a nice, polite boy. From a good Catholic family—his father is an attorney and he was an altar boy. Valentina seems to like him very much."

"She's only seventeen."

Sofia laughed. "Not *that* much. And this is only their first date."

"Where did they go?"

"To a movie. I don't remember which one."

"The boy knows to have her home by midnight?"

"Yes. Roberto, don't worry so much. Valentina and Daniela are good girls—both will be virgins on their wedding nights. As I was, or have you forgotten?"

That night was forever burned into my memory and I said as much. "It's not the girls I worry about. Or teenage boys, either."

"The assaults? There'll be no more if the *demonio* is dead, as you believe."

"No more by him. But there are other predators out there. Too many, these days."

"But not in Santa Rita. *Dios prohibe.*"

"From your lips to God's ear."

LIANE TORREY

IN MY DREAM, MARTIN came into the bedroom and sat next to me on the bed. Bright moonlight shone through the window so I could see him clearly. He was much younger, the age he'd been when we first met at the Fourth of July picnic, the year after I graduated from high school and he moved to Massillon from Cincinnati to take a job with a construction company. His face fuller and unlined, his hazel eyes clear, his hair—the same auburn color as mine—thicker and the cowlick he'd never been able to tame more pronounced. But he wasn't smiling as he had often done back then. He looked lost, miserable.

He took my hand. His was cold, so cold I wanted to pull mine away. But I didn't. "I'm sorry for all the pain I've caused you, Liane."

"I know you are."

"I never meant you to be hurt. Not in any way."

"I know that, too."

"Do you still believe in me, even now?"

"Yes. I never doubted your innocence."

"I wasn't innocent in Ohio. Those terrible things I did—"

"You were sick then. You weren't sick anymore when we came here."

"The police thought I was. Other people. The one who killed me."

"Wrong, they're all so wrong."

"You're better off without me," he said.

"No. No, I'm not."

"You should have divorced me when they sent me to that hospital. You should have started a new life."

"I couldn't leave you at a time like that, even if I'd wanted to. And I didn't want to. My life was with you, for better or worse."

"For worse, then and now. Did you really believe things would be better when we moved out here?"

"Yes. I did."

"The way they were before my sickness? The good times we had then? Picnics, barbecues, dinner parties with friends. The driving trip to St. Louis, the steamboat cruise down the Mississippi."

"I thought we could have good times here, yes. A new place, a fresh start."

"But we didn't, did we. No cruises on this river, no trips anywhere. No picnics or barbecues or dinner parties. No friends."

"Holly and Nick—"

"Neither of them liked me. They only tolerated me for your sake."

"That's not true."

"It is true. You know it is."

"I was starting to make friends, you would have, too, eventually—"

"No, I wouldn't. I used to like people and people liked me. Some people, anyway. But not here. Everyone looked and acted as if they sensed something wrong with me. That's why I kept to myself at work, why I quit Nick's bowling team after three weeks. I told you that. You said you understood."

"I did understand. Things would have gotten better, if . . ."

"If I'd registered as a sex offender as I was supposed to. If my past hadn't caught up with me, if our new life hadn't come apart at the seams."

"I don't blame you for that. Nick couldn't have gotten you the job at Soderholm if they'd known about . . . if they'd known."

"I could have found another job. The police would still have accused me of being a rapist, registered or not."

"It's a monstrous coincidence the rapes started after we moved here. You had nothing to do with them, you couldn't have because . . ."

"Because ever since I got out of the hospital, I was impotent. They wouldn't have believed me if I'd told them. Or you, either."

"It wasn't a permanent condition—"

"Wasn't it?"

"You just needed more time to heal, to adjust."

"You kept saying that. Heal, adjust. 'We've only been here a few months, Marty, give it more time.' Trying to convince me or yourself?"

"You." But that was a lie. Me, too, yes. Yes.

"Even when I could get it up, I couldn't give you a child. But I'm glad I couldn't. You should be glad, too."

"Oh, but I'm not." That was also a lie. I wanted children very much in the beginning, and if I had had a baby, then it would have given me comfort during the long, lonely months Martin was away, but by the time we came to California it was too late and I was no longer sorry we were childless. And now? Now?

"I can't cry for you, Marty," I said. "I want to but I can't."

"I'm not worth crying over," he said. "I never was. I've brought you nothing but pain and misery. I'm better off dead. You're better off too."

"Don't say that."

"You know it's true."

"No, I don't know it. You're a victim, too, violated just like those poor women—"

"It doesn't matter anymore." He let go of my hand and stood up. "Don't grieve too long, Liane. Start over again with somebody new. Somebody like Allan Zacks."

"I don't have any feelings for Allan." Another lie?

"He has feelings for you. He's the kind of man you need, strong, reliable, emotionally stable."

"No . . ."

"Yes."

He backed away from the bed, and a dream mist seemed to be around him, making him look shimmery, indistinct. And then he was gone. He didn't say good-bye, he just vanished into the mist. Gone.

Gone.

I lay there wanting him to come back and not wanting him to come back. And hating myself because I was as glad as I was sad that my life with him was over.

PART TWO

SUNDAY, APRIL 17–
THURSDAY, APRIL 21

GRIFFIN KELLS

SUNDAY MORNING.

Nice one, too, weatherwise. Birds racketing in the pine trees outside, sunlight slanting into the bedroom through the space between the drapery folds.

The kind of day even an overworked, harassed servant of the people ought to be able to enjoy.

When there were no crises to deal with and I wasn't required to appear at some community event, Sundays were reserved for Jenna and me. Once a month we attended church. Neither of us was much taken with formal religion, but Jenna felt, rightly, that it was politic for the chief of police to be seen now and then praying along with the rest of the flock. The other Sundays we'd make love, stay in bed for a while afterward reading the newspapers, then have breakfast at home or brunch out and spend the rest of the day doing whatever we felt like.

This would have been a good Sunday to spend boating on the river, in the small Chris-Craft inboard we kept berthed at the North Park Marina. In the summer months Jenna liked to water-ski. She was good at it, too; she had the willowy body and coordination of a young girl. The water was too cold for skiing this time of year, but on sunny late-April days like this one, it wouldn't be too chilly for a bundled-up boat ride as far south as the Tule Bend marshes. Jenna would have been all for it. Art was another of her talents; she was particularly good at depicting marsh birds in both charcoal sketches and watercolors, and this was the perfect time of year for bird watching and sketching. I'd have liked nothing better today than to let the cold wind and the quiet marsh sloughs clear away some of the overload of stress, sharp this morning after another restless night. Not even two Ambien got me more than four or five hours of sleep these days.

Well, there was one thing I'd have liked better right now. Jenna was still asleep, lying on her side facing toward me. She'd thrown the covers partially off, and the shorty nightgown she wore had hiked up over one slim, bare hip, revealing some of the curly ash-blonde hairs at the shadowed joining of her legs. I felt a stirring of desire, but I didn't do anything about it. There was time enough, but I was too tired, too tense, too distracted, for the kind of slow, leisurely lovemaking we both preferred.

So no sex, and no boat ride, and no pressure-free time with Jenna this Sunday. Nor had there been on many others since the serial rapes turned life in Santa Rita upside down.

I was getting out of bed when Jenna rolled over onto her back, opened the eye nearest me, yawned, then stretched provocatively. When I didn't respond, she said, "Not this morning, huh?"

"Not this morning. Much as I'd like to."

She didn't try to change my mind. Understanding and supportive, as always. I loved her for that and a hundred other things. There is no such thing as a perfect marriage, but ours was about as close to one as you can get. I never tired of looking at her, talking to her, being with her. She excited me as much now as she had the first time I'd set eyes on her, at a Breast Cancer Awareness fund-raiser in Fresno when I was a lieutenant on the FPD. She'd been active then, as she was now, in foundation and charity work and recently divorced from her lazy, good-for-nothing first husband. I was between lady friends, not that it would have mattered if I'd been there with a date instead of my sister and her husband. Instant rapport between us that night. I asked her to marry me on our fourth date; she said yes on our fifth. A fund-raiser is the last place you'd expect two people to meet and fall in love, but the unconventionality made it all the more special.

The only problem we'd had in our nine years together was Jenna's unwillingness to have children. A painful miscarriage during the bad first marriage and the chances of again not being able to carry a baby to term, and concerns about birth defects (one of her brothers had been born with cerebral palsy), were her stated reasons.

I was all for adopting a child, even though it was likely to be a long and time-consuming process. Before the string of assaults began, I thought I had her talked into it, but then she'd backed away again. Too many demands on my time, she'd said, and on hers because of the charity work she was committed to, to pursue an adoption now. But I had the feeling there was more to it than that. That maybe she simply didn't want the responsibility of motherhood . . .

She got out of bed, tugging the nightie down, and reached for her robe. "You go ahead and shower first. I'll start breakfast."

"Just toast and coffee for me. Not much appetite this morning."

"A couple of eggs, too. You need the protein."

I took my shower, and while I was dressing, my cell phone buzzed. Evan Pendergast. Family law attorney, city councilman, and supporter of Mayor Delahunt. Not even nine o'clock, and the pressure was starting again already. He and Councilwoman Aretha Young wanted a meeting "at my earliest convenience." He suggested ten in my office. I could have hurried and gotten down there by then, but I was in no mood to be obliging; I told him eleven was the soonest I could manage it. My relations with the city council were a little shaky now. Pendergast and Young, like Delahunt, were all too eager to place the blame for lack of results directly on my shoulders. Dale Hitchens, owner of the feed mill, and the other three council members were still in my corner, but that could change if we didn't catch a break soon.

Jenna had breakfast ready when I went into the kitchen. Alongside my plate of eggs and toast was the front section of the *Riverton Sentinel*, the county's only daily. "You're in there," she said, "along with the mayor. Page two."

No surprise in that. A reporter and photographer from the *Sentinel* had been the first of the media wolves to show up yesterday, interviewing Delahunt and me among others. An account of the Torrey homicide filled the lower third of the front page, headlined SANTA RITA RAPE

SUSPECT MURDERED; I didn't read it. The photos accompanying the story's continuation on page two were unflattering. Christ. The one of me resembled a mug shot.

"There's an editorial, too," Jenna said. "How long will Santa Rita's reign of terror continue, et cetera. Don't bother reading it."

"I didn't intend to."

"Or Delahunt's usual intimations of police ineptitude. It'll just make you mad."

"Political grandstanding disguised as bureaucratic outrage—he's good at that. Results soon or heads will roll, meaning mine."

"That's about it. I heard you on the phone. Was it Delahunt who called?"

"No. Evan Pendergast." I told her about the eleven o'clock meeting with him and Aretha Young. "More pressure coming up."

"Delahunt had a hand in stirring them up, I'll bet."

"Sure." I tapped the newsprint. "So did what's in here."

"Not everybody's blaming you. Did you see Ted Lowenstein's editorial on the *Clarion* website?"

"No. Not yet."

"He's still firmly on your side. Denounces rushes to judgment by elected officials and takes a few more shots at the mayor. He dislikes Delahunt even more than we do."

"Did he put in a plea for witnesses? He told me he would."

"He did. An impassioned one citing civic and moral duty. Want me to get the laptop?"

"No, I'll read what he has to say later. I'd better get down to the station, see if there are any new developments and check the night-shift reports before I go up against Pendergast and Young."

"If anything important happened, you'd have been notified."

"I know. Still. I need to keep on top of things."

"Eat your eggs before you leave, if they're not already cold."

They were, a little, but I ate them anyway. The toast, too, washed down with a quick cup of coffee. At the door Jenna kissed me hard, held on to me for a few seconds in a tight embrace. My rock. If I didn't have her, the constant strain would have taken an even greater toll on me by now.

ROBERT ORTIZ

JACK SPIVEY AND HIS son were playing catch in their front yard when I drove up. Or rather the boy was pitching and the man catching. A lanky youngster, Timmy Spivey had a nice, easy windup and a smooth delivery for a ten-year-old. A pitcher on his Little League team, I thought, and probably a good one.

They stopped throwing and Spivey scowled at me as I approached. "You again. What now?"

"Suppose we talk alone, Mr. Spivey."

"What about?"

"Alone, please."

He said, "Shit," under his breath, then to his son, "Timmy, go on inside. You can pitch some more after he leaves."

The boy nodded, gave me a narrow-eyed look, and went into the house.

Spivey removed his catcher's mitt, threw it to the ground. He was a big man, heavyset, with a beer belly and beady little eyes half-hidden in pouches of flesh. "Well?" he said.

"I have more questions about your whereabouts on Friday night."

"What questions? I went bowling, like I told you."

"I spoke to two of your teammates this morning. The league you bowl in is an early one, play beginning at seven and ending at approximately nine thirty."

"So?"

"You left immediately after the last game and were not seen again that night. According to your wife, you didn't return home until after she went to bed at eleven o'clock. Where were you between nine thirty and midnight?"

"That's my business."

"Martin Torrey was killed during those hours."

"Chrissake. You trying to say I went to Echo Park?"

"Did you?"

"No!"

"Then where did you go?"

"What'll you do if I don't tell you, arrest me?"

I would not, and he knew it. "Do you have something to hide, Mr. Spivey?"

"Not me. I just don't like cops prying into my private life when there's no call for it."

"There's a call for it. The investigation of a major felony—"

"Felony, hell. A piece of crap flushed down the sewer so it don't cause any more stink."

"A human being murdered in cold blood."

"Jesus Christ. He was a lousy rapist. He raped my wife right here in my house, in my own goddamn bed!"

"There's no excuse for murder in the eyes of the law." *Or for blasphemy on the Sabbath,* I thought, but didn't say.

"How many times I have to tell you I didn't do it? You got no reason to keep hassling me."

"I am not hassling you. I'm asking for your cooperation in a homicide investigation. Tell me where you went and what you did after you left Santa Rita Lanes, and if your answer proves satisfactory, I won't bother you again."

He thrust his jaw out and said belligerently, "No. It's none of your business, Ortiz, or anybody else's but mine. Now suppose you get off my property and leave me the hell alone."

"For the time being. If necessary, I'll be back."

"You do and I'll get a lawyer and sue you and the goddamn city for harassment."

I left him without responding to the threat, which I took to be nothing more than bluster. The man was obviously hiding something, but was it connected to the Torrey slaying? Was he a murderer, or simply a contentious fool?

The county pathologist's report, when it came in tomorrow or Tuesday, might help decide how strongly to pursue Spivey. If it narrowed down the time of death to before eleven Friday night, Spivey was not the shooter; an hour and a half was too narrow a window of time. He might still have had a hand in it, however; more than one individual could be involved. If Torrey had been killed later than ten thirty, and Spivey continued to refuse to divulge his whereabouts, he would be a definite suspect.

I had assigned Karl Simms to interrogate Arthur Pappas and his partner, George Medlock, and Susan Sinclair to do likewise with Eileen Jordan and Courtney Reeves's mother. Their preliminary reports virtually eliminated all four from suspicion. Pappas and Medlock had spent Friday evening at an LGBT event in Riverton and supplied the names of several individuals who could corroborate this. Miss Jordan had been so badly traumatized by her ordeal she could barely function, in Susan's opinion, and Mrs. Reeves satisfactorily accounted for her whereabouts.

Al Bennett was at his desk, just back from interrogating Nicholas Dexter, when I arrived at the station. "Dexter doesn't have an alibi for Friday night," he said. "Home alone watching TV while his wife was at the Cineplex with Mrs. Torrey. But he was Torrey's only friend in Santa Rita, got him his job at Soderholm, claimed all along that he was innocent of the rapes . . . well, you know that. Plus his wife talked him into putting up fifteen hundred of Torrey's bail money, and he was bitching about how now he'd never get any of it back. No motive for homicide that I can see."

Nor could I. Dexter was a weak-willed complainer dominated by his wife, not at all the type to plan and carry out a premeditated homicide. She might have been able to manipulate him into the shooting if she hated Torrey enough for the damage he'd done to her sister, but her belief in Torrey's innocence had seemed genuine, and she had been instrumental in the Torreys' move to Santa Rita. Nor did the abandoned Camry, the riverbank in Echo Park, the postmortem arrangement of the body, fit with a family-related homicide.

Chief Kells was in his office. Al had already reported to him; I went in and did the same.

"Jack Spivey is hiding something, no question of that," I said. "Whether the time gap has anything to do with the homicide depends on the autopsy results. If it turns out Torrey was killed sometime after nine o'clock, I'll put more pressure on Spivey."

"We'll know fairly soon. I got hold of Ed Braverman—at his home, not the lab. County doesn't have enough money to keep the pathology department open six days, let alone seven, even to work on priority cases. I told him it was urgent we have the time of death narrowed down ASAP. He said he'll try to give us a preliminary report tomorrow, but that it'll probably be Tuesday before the autopsy's done. Usual backlog excuse."

"It shouldn't take him more than a few minutes to dig out one of the bullets. Just knowing the caliber will be a help."

"I told him that, too," Griff said. "Same answer. Preliminary report tomorrow . . . maybe."

"We'll have Joe Bloom's report on the Camry in the morning, but I don't expect it will tell us much."

"Neither do I. Even if he finds clear latents belonging to somebody other than Torrey and his family, which is doubtful, it wouldn't help us much. No way to tell how long they'd been in the vehicle."

When I left Griff, I detoured into the property room, picked up the evidence bags containing the contents of Martin Torrey's pockets and the Camry's glove compartment, and took them into my office. I am not fond of writing reports, though I've been told I do them well and thoroughly, and once more sifting through what little evidence we had accumulated was a way of postponing the task. I did not expect to learn anything new.

But when I spread the pocket items on my desk—wallet with fourteen dollars in fives and ones and a photograph of Liane Torrey but no credit cards, forty-five cents in change, key ring, pocketknife—and studied them, there was a nudging at the back of my mind. Something seemed wrong somehow, different.

It was not the absence of Torrey's cell phone. The perp must have taken it, probably because it contained voice mail messages that could be recovered even if erased. There was no way to trace calls made or received on the phone because those owned by both Torrey and his wife were prepaid Walmart throwaways. We could subpoena their landline records, but those would not tell us anything; even if Torrey had communicated with the perp on his home phone, the chances of it being on the day or night of the murder were virtually nil.

What was it that seemed different, then? I had never seen any of these items before they were removed from the body at the crime scene . . .

Yes, I had. The keys on the key ring. When Al Bennett and I had gone to the Torrey home with the search warrants three weeks ago, Torrey had been annoyed enough to hand me the ring instead of unlocking the Camry himself. My memory is good, and I was certain it had contained four keys that day. Now there were only two.

I picked up the ring and examined each. One was for the Camry, clearly labeled with Toyota's logo. The other was most likely his house key.

What had happened to the other two?

One must have been for the Soderholm Brewery delivery van he'd driven, I thought, and he had turned it in when he was fired. And the fourth?

I closed my eyes in an attempt to visualize it. Ordinary silver key, but with one distinctive difference: a small red dot on the round upper portion, just above the hole for ring or chain. I had not paid enough attention to the dot to recall if it was part of the key or had been applied in some way. The dot seemed to rule out a safe-deposit box, and the key had been nothing like the one I carried for Sofia's and mine at the Merchant's Bank. For a padlock? Possibly, though there had been none of any size on the premises. For the rear door of the house? Also possible, but the front-door key was bronze colored and the silver one had been slightly smaller, and there seemed little reason for Torrey to have removed a back-door key from the ring. If in fact it was Torrey who had removed it.

What did the key with the red dot unlock, then? And what had happened to it?

HOLLY DEXTER

LIANE LOOKED BETTER THIS morning, not as pale and with the spark of life in her eyes again. I thought she ought to stay in bed, but, no, she insisted on getting up.

While she was toweling off after her shower, I told her about Allan Zacks's visit and how concerned he was and that he might be coming over again today. I thought it might perk her up. It didn't seem to, much, but maybe it did, because she put on a blouse and skirt instead of her robe and then ran a comb through her hair. She has nice hair, thick and auburn, much nicer than my mousy brown. She never has to fuss with it to get it to look decent, either, the way I do with mine. The short pixie cut is perfect for the shape of her face, too.

I used to envy Liane when we were growing up. Prettier than me, never ill at ease around guys, always getting lots of attention and about twice as many dates as I ever did. Good-looking guys, too, most of them more attractive than Marty. Why she married him instead of Tom Christian or Conner Troy, both handsome jocks, I'll never know. No accounting for taste, I suppose. Look who I married. Not that Nick didn't catch your eye when he was young, but in a sort of ordinary way. He wasn't even the best pick of my small litter, as far as looks and personality go.

But he talked a good fight back then in Ohio, big plans about someday owning a ranch out here in California and raising horses and cattle. I guess he was sincere at the time, only things sure didn't work out that way. The "good job" on a ranch near Santa Rita a friend had told him about was anything but, just long hours and hard work, and it didn't take him long to decide being a rancher wasn't what he wanted after all. Wouldn't you know that of half a dozen other jobs, the only one that lasted was driving a brewery truck. Still, he's a better husband than Marty ever was. Never done anything weird or bad or caused me any real grief. So I guess I'm the lucky sister after all.

Well, anyhow.

Liane wasn't hungry, but I made her eat a few bites of oatmeal and toast to keep her strength up. I tried to make conversation at the table, to keep her mind off what had happened to Marty, but she didn't seem to feel like talking.

The doorbell rang while we were eating and I went to answer it, thinking it might be Allan. But, no, it was some TV person with a microphone, a cameraman, and a request for a brief interview with "the grieving widow." I made short work of him, saying, "Mrs. Torrey has nothing to say to the media," before I shut the door in his face.

After I washed the dishes and made Liane's bed, we sat in the living room. She didn't want to talk then, either. The quiet got to me after a while and I suggested turning on the TV, but she said she preferred it quiet. But she didn't seem to be brooding or lost inside herself the way she'd been yesterday, which was a relief.

"You really don't have to stay here with me, Holly," she said then. "I'll be all right."

"I don't think you should be alone yet."

"Don't worry, I'm not going to fall apart."

"But I do worry. I'll just stay through the afternoon. Keep the wolves away from the door."

And off the phone, too. Her landline rang twice, another media jerk the first time and then some anonymous asshole who thought I was Liane and said how glad he was "that dirty rapist husband of yours is dead." I told him to go screw himself and slammed the phone down. It was the kitchen extension, so Liane didn't hear me. A good thing I'd answered it and not her.

Another call came at one o'clock, this one on my cell. Nick wanting to know how Liane was and to tell me he'd had a visit from a cop named Bennett. "Asked me a bunch of questions about Friday night and about my relationship with Marty," he said.

"My God. Don't tell me they think you're a suspect?"

"No. Hell, no. He said they're talking to everybody who knew him or might've had a motive for shooting him."

"Well, that's good," I said. "Maybe they'll actually find out who did it. You were cooperative, weren't you?"

"Sure, I was cooperative. I'm not stupid."

"What did you say about Marty?"

"The same things you'd've said if you were here. That I always got along with him and I don't think he committed those rapes and I'm sorry he's dead."

"Did he believe you?"

"Well, it's the truth, isn't it? Christ." Nick made one of his whistling sighs. "Liane need you to spend the night there again?"

"I don't think so. I'll probably be home around dinnertime."

"Good. You're a lot better cook than I am."

That was Nick for you. Always thinking of himself, even in the midst of a crisis.

Allan finally called at two o'clock. How was Liane and would it be all right if he stopped by to see her around four? I checked with her to make sure she didn't mind. She didn't, which was encouraging. I'd leave for home when he came, I decided. He had a quiet, reassuring way about him—a sort of soothing dentist's bedside manner, if there is such a thing. Chair-side manner? Well, whatever. I'd done all I could for her for the time being. Maybe he could do something to lift her spirits a little more.

He arrived at four on the dot. He had on a suit and tie and looked positively scrumptious, even with the grave expression he wore in place of his usual smile. This was no time to be thinking about such things, but I hoped they'd be more than just employer and employee one day. They'd make a handsome couple. And he'd be so good for her, so much better than Marty had been. She deserved some happiness, some real happiness, after what she'd been through the past couple of years.

I showed Allan into the living room and stayed just long enough to tell Liane I was leaving. But I didn't leave, not for quite a while. I was getting my coat out of the hall closet when the doorbell rang. Another media jerk, I thought, but, no, it was the big Mexican cop, Lieutenant Ortiz.

"I'd like to speak to Mrs. Torrey."

I glared at him. "What for? Can't you leave her to grieve in peace for one day?"

"I have a few more questions."

"Questions, questions. Why do you have to keep persecuting her?"

"I am not persecuting her, Mrs. Dexter. I am trying to find out who murdered her husband."

"She doesn't know anything about what happened to Martin, she told you that yesterday. Besides, she has a visitor, somebody else who cares about her. Dr. Allan Zacks."

"I won't take up much of her time. Or yours. Or Dr. Zacks's."

God, he was an exasperating man. But what could I do except let him in? If I didn't, he'd just come back again later and probably make things even harder on Liane.

Allan stood up, frowning, when I brought Ortiz into the living room. Liane didn't move or show any surprise that the big bulldog was back again so soon with more questions and no apology. Allan didn't like him bothering her, that was plain from his expression, but he couldn't do anything about it, either. He said, "Do you want me to leave the room while you ask your questions?" When Ortiz said it wasn't necessary, Allan went over next to Liane's chair and stood there in a sort of protective way. I liked him even more for doing that.

"All right, Lieutenant," she said in a dull voice. "What is it this time?"

"A matter of a missing key."

"What missing key?"

"From your husband's key ring. It held four keys when the search of his vehicle was made three weeks ago. Now there are only two."

"That's two keys gone," I said, "not one."

"The other can be accounted for. For the brewery truck he drove while he was employed there. It's the fourth I'm interested in."

"Why, for heaven's sake? What does a key have to do with anything."

Ortiz ignored me. "Silver," he said to Liane, "with a small red dot above the ring hole. Familiar?"

"No. I never paid any attention to Martin's keys."

Who does? I thought. A key is a key. One of mine could have had pink polka dots on it and I probably wouldn't have noticed.

"Do you have any idea what he might have used it for?"

"No."

Ortiz looked at me. "Mrs. Dexter?"

"How would I know anything about Martin's keys? My husband might, but I doubt it. Call him up and ask him. He's home."

"Before I do that," Ortiz said, looking at Liane again, "I'll check among your husband's effects. If you have no objection?"

Allan said, "I don't see how this allegedly missing key pertains to your investigation."

"It may not. I won't know until I find out why he carried it and why it's no longer on his key ring."

Allan started to say something more, then changed his mind. He had a pinched look on his face now, as if something he didn't like had just occurred to him. Well, I thought I knew what it was because I'd just had the same thought. Great minds and all that. Ortiz didn't believe the missing key had anything to do with Marty's murder; he was looking for it because he thought it might prove his obsessive theory that Marty had raped those poor women. The mask, gloves, and knife the rapist used had never been found, and to Ortiz's nasty way of thinking that missing key might open a box or something where they were hidden. But I kept my mouth shut just as Allan had. Liane was upset enough as it was without having that damned can of worms opened up again.

She said in that same dull voice, "If I say no, you'll just get another search warrant. So go ahead, look all you want, anywhere you want. I don't care."

"Mrs. Dexter, will you come with me, please?"

"Do I have a choice? Oh, all right."

I went with him into their bedroom and stood around fuming while Ortiz rummaged through Marty's few belongings. He didn't find the key with the red dot in the bedroom or the bathroom or anywhere else in the house. I thought that would be the end of it, but no, he had to go out and look in the garage, too. He poked around in there for ten minutes, opening up cabinets and cartons. Fat lot of good it did him. The missing key wasn't anywhere on the property, unless somebody had buried it in the yard. I wouldn't put it past him to have a team of cops come in and dig up every inch of ground.

When he was finally satisfied, we didn't go straight back into the house. Oh, no, I had to stand out in the yard with him while he called Nick on his cell and asked him about the key. Nick didn't know anything about it, either. I could tell that from Ortiz's end of the conversation.

Then we went inside, Ortiz just long enough to tell Liane he hadn't found the damn key and to let him know if she remembered anything about it. When he was gone, she said, "He'll be back," in that same dull voice.

"He'd better not," I said.

"He will. There's only one thing that will make him leave me alone."

Allan and I looked at each other. We both knew she didn't mean the police finding out who killed Marty, she meant another woman being attacked, but neither of us said anything. I didn't want a terrible thing like that to happen, God knows, but I didn't want Liane to go on suffering and being hassled, either.

Effing cops. How could they catch the rapist and Marty's murderer by going around looking for keys with red dots?

SHERRY WILDER

As soon as Neal left for his office on Monday morning, I showered and put on black slacks and a loose pullover, the clothes I always wore for my weekly trips to the Bull's-Eye in Riverton. This would be my sixth and I felt energized and eager, as always. Amused, too, because Neal still had no idea what I'd been doing, no clue about my Pink Lady. He'd be furious if he found out, the way he felt about gun control. I used to feel that way, too, but my God, not anymore.

I certainly wasn't going to tell him, and if I was careful, he'd never find out. We'd made a pact when we were married never to poke around in each other's personal possessions, and we'd both honored it. Not once had he ever opened a purse of mine without being asked to. A couple of times recently he'd picked up and handed me the big Baggallini Bagg he'd given me for Christmas two years ago, when Christmas was still a white and not a black holiday for me, but he hadn't had an inkling that the ultralightweight Pink Lady was nestled deep inside. She weighed only twelve ounces.

Before I left the house I opened the bag and took her out, as I sometimes did when Neal wasn't around—just for the pleasure of looking at her, holding her. Oh, she was a beauty. Compact, five-shot .38 Undercover Special. Two-tone aluminum frame, anodized hot pink and stainless. Two-inch barrel, fixed sights, soft rubber grips, and a three-point cylinder lock. She felt just right gripped in my hand, and she fired effortlessly once you got used to her. Hardly any recoil at all. Made for women, perfect for women.

I'd bought her in the Bull's-Eye gun store. But only after I'd taken their Women's Academy safety seminar and training course and learned the basic principles of self-defense and how to handle and fire a handgun, then got a permit. Before going to Bull's-Eye, I had never shot one, never even held one. Their certified women's instructor, Tina Collins, also taught the proper use of OC pepper spray and gave me a free can when I completed the course. Naturally I kept it in the Baggallini with the Pink Lady.

At first, on the range, Tina had me fire different types and calibers of guns to find out which I was most comfortable with. Basic Pistol, training and practice, this course was called. Once I passed it, I was allowed to buy a gun of my own. I fell in love with the Pink Lady as soon as I saw her. And we performed together beautifully from the first. Now after five sessions I was in Intermediate Pistol, where you focused on close-grouping your shots at various distances.

I couldn't wait to get to Bull's-Eye and I drove a little faster on the freeway than I should have. I really looked forward to these practice sessions, the way I used to look forward to working out on the treadmills and elliptical cross-trainers at Norden's. That they were a secret from Neal made them even more special.

Tina was free when I arrived and targets were open in the shooting area so I didn't have to wait. I put on the required eye and ear protection, and then the Pink Lady and I spent a glorious hour and a half of close-grouping target practice. My eye was particularly good and my hand perfectly steady today.

Tina thought so, too. "You're becoming very proficient, Sherry." We'd been on a first-name basis since my second session. She was a stocky redhead in her forties, probably a lesbian (not that that mattered to me in the slightest), and an expert markswoman as well as an expert teacher. "Your last half dozen groupings are outstanding."

"Do you think I'm ready to move to the next level?" The next level was Advanced Pistol, where you learned techniques employed in tactical/defensive situations.

"Yes, definitely."

"First lesson next week?"

"Next week it is."

I could have hugged her. If others hadn't been nearby, maybe I would have.

Before leaving Bull's-Eye I carefully cleaned the Pink Lady and polished her aluminum frame and stubby barrel until they gleamed. I felt almost euphoric on the drive back to Santa Rita; it had been a wonderful morning, with the promise of more and even better ones to come. Nothing else had made me feel this good in as long as I could remember. Not running or working out at the gym. Not sex—I'd never liked it all that much with Neal or any other man. Not Johnnie Walker, either, although he was the closest after Bull's-Eye and Tina and the Pink Lady.

I took the downtown exit off the freeway and drove along the river. Norden's was up this way. Maybe I ought to stop in and talk to Sam Norden, I thought. It was time I started working out again, giving fitness lessons again part-time . . . wasn't it? Yes, probably. Sam had come to visit twice after what happened in the park, once in the hospital and once at home, and both times he'd said I was welcome back anytime I was ready, at an increased salary and no charge for my workouts. But I didn't feel like talking to him today. Or to anybody, now that I was back from Riverton. The euphoria was wearing off, the scar on my neck beginning to throb again, and I didn't feel like working out or driving any more or going home yet.

The Santa Rita Inn was just ahead. I turned into the parking lot and went inside, into the bar off the lobby. Three men in suits were perched on stools at the other end, and they all looked at me as I sat down. Well, let them look. Let any man look, as long as that was all he did. None of them better ever again try to stuff their goddamn wienies into me. They'd meet the Pink Lady if they did, up close and personal.

"Johnnie Walker Black Label, neat," I told the bartender. "Make it a double."

GRIFFIN KELLS

WE HAD THE PRELIMINARY forensic report late Monday afternoon, but I had to call and pester Ed Braverman again to get it. The delay was because one of his assistants was out sick and Ed was swamped with work.

Martin Torrey had been shot with a .38-caliber weapon of undetermined manufacture. Without the weapon that had fired it, the information was of no immediate value; .38 was a common handgun caliber. The perp had either carried the piece away with him or chucked it into the river. In the latter case, the chances of recovering it were virtually nonexistent. Even if I could get permission to have a portion of the river in the vicinity of the crime scene dragged—an unlikely prospect given the cost and the uncertainty that that was what had been done with the weapon—it would have been a waste of time. The river was loaded with silt, its bottom all thick, sucking mud. You could drag for something as large as a truck tire you knew was in there somewhere and never find it.

The forensic exam of Torrey's body, clothing, and shoes had revealed one item of interest—a reddish-brown hair on the cuff of a shirtsleeve. But the shirt had been freshly laundered, and the hair color matched that of Torrey's wife; in all likelihood it would turn out to be hers. Otherwise, Braverman had found no worthwhile trace evidence, just grass stems and grass stains and mud from the riverbank on the shoe soles.

The autopsy was still scheduled for Tuesday, time as yet unspecified, but if the assistant didn't show up again, Braverman said, it might not get done until Wednesday. Hurry up and wait, like the goddamn military. We needed a better estimate of the time of death.

Braverman confirmed the cause as a single bullet fired at close range into the brain through the left temple, the slug lodging against the parietal bone to prevent exit. The two in the groin had been administered postmortem. There was powder tattooing on the trousers as well, he told me, so those rounds had also been fired point-blank.

Joe Bloom's report was even less revealing than Braverman's. The only clear latent prints in the Camry were Martin Torrey's, all others smudges and overlaps. Careful vacuuming of the carpets produced nothing other than the usual dirt, dust, pollen, plant and grass fibers.

We'd had no luck in finding witnesses to the incidents on Friday night. Not that this was any surprise. Very few vehicles venture through the South Street industrial area after dark. Some homeless were known to bed down in the area, but they were law-leery; none that my men talked to would admit to having seen anything.

Torrey and his killer had probably entered Echo Park near where the body was found, which meant that the vehicle that had transported them there had been parked in that vicinity—on Parkside Drive, the street that paralleled the outer edge of the park, or on one of the streets that led off it into the housing development there. The drive's east side was lined with vehicles 24-7, and it would have taken only a few seconds when there was no traffic to cross into the park. I'd had a team canvass the homes in the immediate area, but none of the residents had noticed anything out of the ordinary. Neither had any of the officers who night-patrolled Echo Park and vicinity.

So once again we were mired in frustration. No solid evidence. No witnesses. And no suspects except for Jack Spivey—if the approximate time of death was eleven or later, and if he couldn't or wouldn't adequately account for his whereabouts after leaving Santa Rita Lanes.

JENNA KELLS

THE PAINTING WASN'T GOING well. I was trying to do a watercolor of a long-billed curlew I'd sketched in charcoal last summer, and I couldn't seem to get it right. The sketch was all right, but the colors of the bird's plumage and the surrounding marshland weren't. Too pale, the pastels washed-out instead of properly representational. The painting simply wouldn't come *alive*.

I gave it up after a while. Not a good day to be engaging in passive pursuits, with all the upheaval in Santa Rita and Griff smack in the middle of it. Worrying about him made me restless, edgy. I wished this were one of my days for volunteer work—the Breast Cancer Awareness program, art classes at the seniors' home, assistance at the county food bank. But it wasn't. And you could only do so much.

No, that was a cop-out. There was always more you could do, so many worthwhile charities, so many needy people. And not just by giving money but by donating time as well. Children, for instance. Disadvantaged children, hearing-impaired children, autistic and Down's syndrome children. Children afflicted with cerebral palsy like my younger brother Paul. Griff had suggested a number of times that I volunteer for a child-oriented charity, and once without telling him I'd made the effort. Volunteered part-time at a camp for kids with Down's syndrome . . . and lasted less than two weeks. A painful experience, very. The problem I'd had was not too little empathy but too much; I'd felt like weeping the entire time I was there.

I liked children, I really did, but I couldn't help being ambivalent about having a child of my own. Couldn't help being afraid. Of another miscarriage and the physical and mental anguish it caused. Of a baby's being born with a severe birth defect like Down's, a real possibility for a woman my age, or cerebral palsy like Paul. Of the changes the demands of parenthood would bring to an orderly, comfortable lifestyle. And of the increasingly chaotic world we lived in, evidence of which I faced every day in the details and stresses of Griff's job. Bringing a child into such an unstable and violent environment seemed somehow irresponsible, almost cruel.

Fears, Jenna? Or rationalizations, excuses?

Griff wanted so much to be a father, and I hated to keep disappointing him. I'd almost let him talk me into adopting, if not having a baby of our own, but then the series of violent rapes started. Those poor women, so much pain and suffering . . . I'd backed off again. Now . . .

Now I needed to stop brooding and get out of this house, do something constructive that involved interaction with others. It wasn't my day at the seniors' home, but there was no reason why I couldn't go there anyway. They were understaffed, they always needed volunteers.

I put on my coat and went out to the car, leaving all my painting and sketching tools behind. Whatever I could do at the home today, it would be more beneficial than teaching the rudiments of art.

EILEEN JORDAN

I WENT SHOPPING AT Safeway this morning and it was as if I weren't there at all.

No one looked at me as I pushed my cart up and down the aisles, through the frozen-food and canned-goods and housewares and produce sections. No one spoke to me. I didn't stop at the meat-and-fish counter, but if I had, I felt that I would not have been served because none of the butchers would have noticed me waiting. The invisible woman. Not even a shadow of her former self, not that her former self had cast much of a shadow, either.

There was more to the sense of unreality. It was not just as if I had become invisible, it was as if the sentient part of me had separated from my body and I functioned in an interactive dream state, watching my invisible self picking items off shelves and putting them into the cart, pushing the cart into the checkout lane, placing my purchases on the conveyor belt, paying an unseeing checker with a credit card. Watching while I participated, my tactile and olfactory senses intact. The chill of frozen dinners, the hardness of cans, the softness of vegetables; the odor of roasted chicken, the scent of fresh herbs, the tang of oranges.

I have only vague memories of driving to the supermarket, driving back home again. I must have been aware enough to make both trips safely, but when I was inside the house again, it was as if I had never left.

Three bags of groceries sat on the kitchen table; I must have carried them in from the car, but I had no recollection of it.

The feeling of unreality left me as I unloaded the bags and put the items away in the refrigerator, the bread box, the cabinets next to the sink. I was myself again. Whole again, or as whole as I would ever be. It was as if the world outside no longer existed for me. As if my part in it, my reality, had narrowed to these three drab rooms.

When had I last eaten? I couldn't remember—sometime yesterday, and then only a little soup. I was aware of rumblings in my stomach, hunger pangs, but the thought of food, any kind of food, nauseated me. Tea, juice, broth . . . not any of those, either.

I went once more to sit in Grandmother's rocker. I spent more and more time there, looking at nothing, hardly even thinking so as to avoid flashback memories of the invasion. After my experience at Safeway, I was not sure I could bring myself to leave the cottage again for any reason. I had no interest in anything anymore, it seemed. Not teaching. Not reading or gardening or walking in the park or visiting with Barbara or any of the other simple pleasures that had occupied my time for so many years. All I cared to do was sit here rocking, rocking, rocking.

Would reality contract even more, from the three drab rooms to this chair alone? Would I then just sit here all day and all night, unwilling or unable to move, wasting away, fading until I was no longer even a shadow, no longer here either anymore?

I mustn't let that happen. Yet there does not seem to be any way to prevent it.

TED LOWENSTEIN

JUDGING FROM THE INITIAL responses to our website posts, a fairly large percentage of our benevolent citizens were satisfied that Martin Torrey had gotten what he deserved, whether he was the serial rapist or not. E-mails were running about 20 percent along those lines. One bigoted idiot even went so far as to write that all sex offenders, no matter what their specific crimes, "should be killed along with all the rest of the fags and felons so decent people can sleep nights." I turned that one over to Griff Kells, but nothing had come of it. Apparently the writer was nothing more than a dim-witted crank.

Most correspondents remained supportive of Kells's and his department's efforts, and of the *Clarion*'s stance in their favor. A few—hell, more than a few—took exception to my most recent anti-Delahunt editorial, but that was nothing new; he still had a lot of backers in Santa Rita, among them his brother-in-law, Councilman Pendergast, Councilwoman Young, and the other prominent dunderheads who'd helped put him in office.

I kept telling myself I was making inroads among the voters, changing enough minds to get him defeated if he ran for another term as mayor or, more likely, for the county board of supervisors. But that wasn't necessarily the case. In my younger days I subscribed 100 percent to Lincoln's famous quote about not being able to fool all the people all of the time. Now, in my cynical middle age, I've begun to think that Mencken's equally famous line about never underestimating the intelligence of the great masses of plain people is more on target. Particularly where politics is concerned.

I was in a short-tempered mood today, made worse by a harassing phone call from one of the mayor's cronies on the county board of supervisors. I hung up on him midway through his pro-Delahunt, anti-Kells, anti-Lowenstein harangue. Shortly afterward the Smith kid turned in a late, crappy account of the latest loss by the Santa Rita high school basketball team, and I dressed him down about it in front of the other reporters—something I wouldn't have done if I had been in a better frame of mind. I snapped at a couple of other staff members, blue-penciled the wording in a forthcoming display ad, turned thumbs down on Phil Goldstein's flower show photos and ordered him to reshoot. A good thing this wasn't one of Angela's days at the office or I might have taken out my frustration on her, too.

Frustration is what it was, pure and simple. Too much happening in too short a time, with no resolution in sight. For some members of the media, the kind of ongoing "hot news" that was happening in Santa Rita was a godsend; they milked it for all it was worth, using the "public's right to know" mantra as an excuse to further careers. Not me. One thing I could say for myself: despite my cynicism, despite all the irritants and tumult, my journalistic integrity remained intact. And would stay that way as long as I owned the *Clarion*, as long as I still had a pulse.

LIANE TORREY

I KEPT TELLING MYSELF it was too soon to be doing this, but I kept on doing it just the same. Emptying the dresser drawers of Martin's shirts, socks, underwear, pajamas. Emptying the closets of his one suit, slacks, work pants, jackets, ties, belts, work shoes, dress shoes. Emptying the nightstand drawers, the medicine cabinet, his portion of our shared jewelry box. Emptying the living room shelves of the team bowling trophy he'd won in Massillon, the wood-and-stone clock he'd bought at a flea market, the few other items of little or no value he'd deemed worthy of display.

Emptying the last vestiges of him from my life.

I justified it in two ways. The chore had to be done sooner or later, so why put it off, why keep all the reminders of him to make me feel even more despondent? And it kept me busy, kept me from moping around, brooding, because I had nothing else to occupy my time right now.

Holly had insisted on taking care of the funeral arrangements. Not that there would be any funeral or burial or even a coffin to pick out. Martin's shell would be cremated in a pine box, per his wishes. I would not keep his ashes in an urn, as some people did with their loved ones' cremains. That sort of thing had always seemed morbid to me, a constant . . . what was the phrase? Memento mori. Reminder of death. His would be scattered somewhere by Nick or Holly, someone other than me. Ashes to ashes.

Ashes.

Allan wanted me to come back to work. His temporary hygienist wasn't doing a good job, he said, though that was probably an exaggeration for my benefit, and the sooner I reestablished a semblance of normalcy, the healthier it would be for me. He was right in theory, but I wasn't ready yet to face his parade of patients, people who would ask questions, make accusations with their eyes if not their mouths. I told him I needed more time to regain my equilibrium, at least another week. He understood. He's a very understanding man.

Holly says he's in love with me. Martin thought so, too, enough to be cryptically if not actively jealous. Maybe Allan is, I don't know. It doesn't matter right now whether he is or not. Or exactly what my feelings are toward him. It might never matter. I don't know that I could ever love another man, marry again, put the kind of trust into a relationship that I put into mine with Martin. I just don't know.

All of Martin's belongings went into four of the cartons we'd used for our move from Ohio. He had saved them, flattened and string tied, in a corner of the garage. "Just in case we have to move again," he'd said. I found some box tape and put six back together, but four were all that were needed. He hadn't had many possessions. Thirty-four years old, ten years of marriage, and all that he owned fit into four medium-size shipping cartons.

The only items I couldn't bring myself to get rid of were our silver-framed wedding picture and the two thin photograph albums. I had to keep something to remember him by, didn't I? To remember what our life had been like before his arrest and conviction and sentence to the psychiatric facility.

He looked so happy in the wedding photo, in the other photos Nick had taken at the reception. So did I. Smiling while we cut the cake, smiling at Mom and Dad and the handful of other guests, smiling at each other. I couldn't bear to part with those, especially the ones with my parents in them—they were the last I had of them together before Dad died of a heart attack the following year and colon cancer killed Mom the year after that. All the rest were candid snaps from the good years, the hopeful years. There were no photos of our time in Santa Rita. Not a single one.

I took the framed picture and the albums into the bedroom and put them on a shelf in the closet. Maybe one day I would I take the wedding photo out and set it up where I could look at it again. But not here, not in this house.

I wondered again how long it would be before I could move. The lease had another five months to run. Under the circumstances the landlord might let me break it without a penalty, but then again he might not. I hadn't heard from him, and I hadn't called because I was afraid of what he would say. Five more months in this place, with all its painful memories like lingering ghosts, would be the same as a prison sentence. But I would endure them if I had to, as I had endured everything else. Endurance, a cousin to resignation, was a hard lesson learned the past two years.

I carried the boxes, one by one, out to Holly's Subaru wagon. She'd insisted I use it as long as the Camry remained in police impound. Nick hadn't liked the idea of her taking over his pickup, driving him to work in the morning and picking him up at night when he couldn't catch another ride, but it wasn't much of an inconvenience, and besides, she ruled their roost. More wondering: Would things have been different between Martin and me if I'd tried to rule ours?

Probably not. It was a moot point anyhow. I wasn't made the way Holly was, always needing to be in control. Neither was Martin, for that matter. The passive, nonconfrontational equality we'd shared had suited both our personalities.

With the rear seats folded down, three of the cartons filled the back of the wagon. I wedged the other one into the passenger seat in front. Then I went into the garage to look around. Not much was there, other than a few stored items that I didn't feel like sifting through. And Martin's bowling ball and shoes in a box under the workbench. Bowling—another activity he'd lost interest in. Nobody would want a used ball and shoes, so I left them where they were.

There was a hospice thrift store less than a mile from the house. They took everything, one of the employees helping me unload the cartons. And that was the end of it. The last remnants of Martin James Torrey given away to an organization dedicated to helping the terminally ill die with dignity. In a grim kind of way, it seemed fitting that they should go there.

HUGH DELAHUNT

CRAIG AND I WERE having lunch at the country club, on the terrace overlooking the first tee. This fine spring day, warm and clear, was perfect for golf, and the links were crowded. He had suggested that we play a round, nine holes if not eighteen, and I'd have liked nothing better, but it wouldn't have looked right for me to be openly enjoying myself with the Torrey murder still fresh in people's minds. I was not about to give Lowenstein any more fodder.

Tuesday's *Clarion* lay on the table next to my shrimp salad. I jabbed a finger at the editorial. "I'd like to wring his goddamn neck."

"It's not that bad," Craig said. "He doesn't say anything he hasn't said before."

"It's not what he says, it's what he implies. That I'm weak, ineffectual, that I was a poor lawyer turned political-hack mayor with nobody's best interests at heart but my own. If he keeps this up, he could do me some damage. You know that as well as I do."

"Take it easy, Hugh. You worry too much."

I smiled at him, the smile I use on the media. Craig is a loyal friend and a good husband to my sister Katherine, and I like him well enough, but he's neither savvy nor intuitive. Just a big bearlike nebbish, too easygoing for his own good. Soderholm Brewery was a solid enterprise when he inherited it from his father, and a good thing, too, that it practically ran itself because he had little business acumen and no ambition. A shrewd businessman could have expanded the operation and doubled its profits by now.

"Yes, I do worry too much," I said. "And with good cause. Those rapes and now this murder reflect badly on me. If Lowenstein has his way, they'll become a permanent black mark on my record."

"I suppose you're right."

"Damn right I'm right."

"Well," Craig said slowly, "we could always do what we talked about before. Pull my advertising, get Evan Pendergast to pull his."

I took a sip of my iced tea. Blah. What I really wanted was a double Tanqueray martini, but it wouldn't look good, either, for me to be seen drinking alcohol in the middle of the day.

"No," I said. "That would only give Lowenstein more ammunition for his crusade against me. Too much chance of a voter backlash."

"Just threaten to pull the advertising, then. Give him an ultimatum: lay off or else."

"Use your head, Craig. That kind of tactic would have even more dire consequences. Lowenstein isn't a man you can threaten. He'd get his back up and mount an even stronger attack. Come right out in one of his frigging editorials and accuse me, you, Pendergast, of attempted extortion."

"So then, we're between a rock and a hard place. I don't see any other way to fight him."

"Oh, there's another way," I said. "A way to turn things around to my advantage, make him look bad in the public eye."

"How?"

"Situational leverage."

"What does that mean?"

"Lowenstein strongly supports Chief Kells, doesn't he? Even though Kells and his IU have failed miserably in solving either the rapes or the Torrey murder."

"So far."

"Yes, and I don't see that changing in the immediate future. As long as we've got a murderer running around loose in our midst, the more incompetent Kells looks. And that makes Lowenstein look bad by extension—backing a loser whose ineptitude continues to put the citizens of Santa Rita at risk."

Craig rubbed a hand back and forth across his forehead, as if trying to massage his thought processes into some semblance of clarity. "How does that get him off your back?"

"Situational leverage, like I said. Not with Lowenstein directly, with the members of the city council who continue to back Kells."

"I still don't get it."

Sometimes Craig could be remarkably dense. I swallowed an irritated sigh. "If Torrey's murderer isn't identified and arrested soon, very soon, you and Evan and Aretha and I will put pressure on those council members to do some housecleaning at the PD, fire Kells and Ortiz, promote Frank Judkins to chief and Charlie Eversham to lieutenant. Men sympathetic to my position."

"Okay. But suppose they can't solve the murder, either?"

"That's not the point of this discussion. The point is Lowenstein and how to neutralize his threat to me. Removing Kells won't stop the little pit bull from attacking me in print, but the voters will stop listening to him. Wrong about Kells, wrong about Hugh Delahunt."

"Sure. Now I get it. You really think it'll work?"

"If Kells and Ortiz keep on failing, it will."

Craig drank some of his red wine. Brewery owner drinking wine in public instead of his own product. I'd talked to him about that before, how it looked to people, but it hadn't sunk in. Wine was his tipple, he said, he didn't even like beer. My God, why couldn't Katherine have picked a husband who wasn't "narrow between the ears," as my father used to say. Craig's only saving grace was that he was malleable.

"I guess you're right, Hugh," he said. "But it seems like a pretty unpleasant thing to hope for."

"What does?"

"The rapist not being caught, Torrey's murderer not being caught."

"There won't be any more rapes," I said. "The murderer solved that problem."

"You sound like you wouldn't mind if he got away with it."

"That's not so. You know I don't condone vigilante violence."

And I didn't, naturally, though a reasonable case could be made that Torrey's killer had done us all a favor last Friday night and ought not to be prosecuted for it. Not that I would ever make such a claim, of course, to anyone other than myself.

ROBERT ORTIZ

I COULD NOT GET that missing key out of my mind.

No one seemed to be aware of its existence except me, much less to know what had happened to it or what the red dot signified. Al Bennett thought it might not even exist. "You could be misremembering where you saw the red-dot key," he said. "Or the number of keys on Torrey's ring." But I was not misremembering. There had been four keys three weeks ago, now there were only two. And one of those missing had the dot.

The other missing key definitely had been for the Soderholm delivery van Torrey had driven. I checked with the brewery and verified that it had been reclaimed when he was fired. Since none of his family apparently had any idea what the red-dot key unlocked, it was logical to assume that it opened something that belonged only to Torrey, private property known only to him.

That it had disappeared seemed to have no relevance to the homicide. Yet I had the feeling that there was some sort of connection. And that it was connected to the assaults, too. We had found no sign of the serial's tools—ski mask, gloves, knife—or the stolen handgun anywhere on the Torrey property or among his possessions. If I was right about him, he would have stashed them where he could lay hands on them easily and quickly, some place safe from accidental discovery.

But where? Keys opened or operated hundreds of different kinds of things. Padlocks, cabinets, doors, windows, strongboxes, lockers, vehicles . . . the list was endless. A rapist's Pandora's box could be anything, anywhere, within the city limits.

The missing key was yet another in the string of puzzling elements about the homicide. I had made a list of them and the questions they raised:

The location of the shooting. Why Echo Park, a place regularly patrolled at night? There were other, much more isolated places along the river, in the farmland across it to the north, in the nearby hills.

The location of the Camry. Why abandon it in an industrial section five miles from the scene of the crime?

The position of the body. Why arrange it in that blasphemous posture after death?

And the key. No matter what it opened, why had it been removed from Torrey's key ring?

None of it seemed to make much sense, individually or collectively. Yet I was convinced, and Griff Kells agreed, that there was a pattern here. Answer one of the questions and the other answers would follow, the pattern emerge. Then we would know who had shot Torrey and why.

I was studying the list again for the dozenth time, and still getting nowhere, when Griff called me into his office late Tuesday afternoon. "I just got off the phone with Ed Braverman," he said. "The autopsy's finally done and he's narrowed down the time of death for us. Torrey died sometime between nine and ten Friday night."

"Braverman is sure?"

"As sure as he can be from all the test results. That lets out Jack Spivey. Whatever he was doing after he left the bowling alley, it wasn't murdering Martin Torrey."

IONE SPIVEY

WE WERE OUT OF beer and Jack likes one or two when he gets home from work, so I went to the store around five to buy a couple of six-packs of Bud Light. His pickup was in the driveway when I got back. He and Timmy were in his man cave—I could hear them talking as I came into the kitchen. They must not have heard me because whatever they were chattering about went on without pause. I opened a can of beer, put the rest in the fridge, and carried the open one back to the den.

The door wasn't quite shut so I pushed it open and walked in. And got such a shock that I stopped dead still, my eyes opening wide and my heart skipping two or three beats.

Timmy was standing there holding and pointing the biggest, ugliest gun I'd ever seen in my life. And Jack was right beside him, grinning in a proud kind of way.

"Timmy! What on earth are you—Put that thing down!"

He didn't, he just kept pointing it, squinting down the long barrel. It was so heavy he had to stand with his legs braced wide to hold it steady. He didn't even look at me.

"Don't worry," Jack said, "it's not loaded."

"Make him put it *down*."

"Don't give me orders." Jack's grin was upside down now. "You're not supposed to come barging in here without knocking, you know that."

"I didn't barge in, I only—"

"Never mind. I was just showing Timmy how to hold the piece, that's all. No big deal. Here, kid, let me have it."

Timmy didn't want to let go. His face was a little flushed and his eyes were bright, shiny, like a bird's eyes. Jack had to practically pull the gun out of his hands.

"What is that thing?"

"It's not a thing," Timmy said, "it's a Robinson XCR-L assault weapon. The kind soldiers and cops use. Cool, man! The coolest."

"Assault weapon. That's illegal in California."

"Stupid frigging law." Jack laid it down on the table next to his chair. "You can buy and own a piece like this in other states, so why not here?"

"Where on earth did you get it?"

"Bought it off a guy I know. Hell of a good price, too."

"How much?"

"Never mind how much. Not more than we can afford."

"When? How long have you had it?"

"Since Friday night. I went to the guy's house after bowling to close the deal."

"It's gas-piston fired," Timmy said, "chambered for five-point-five-six NATO ammo. Fires hundreds of rounds a minute, right, Dad?"

"Right."

"My God," I said.

"Yeah," Timmy said. "Wow. Whole bunch of guys coming at you, you just squint down those tactical sights and cut 'em all in half before they know what hit 'em."

My stomach was all clenched up. I tasted bile in the back of my throat. "Jack, what do you want with a . . . a combat weapon like this?"

"Protection, what else."

"Protection against what? An invasion?"

"Could happen. Who the hell knows these days?"

"Dad's thinking of buying a couple more pieces like this," Timmy said. "Maybe three or four."

"What?" I said. "For God's sake, Jack—"

"Thinking about it, that's right," he said. "More of these babies you own, the safer you are."

"That's crazy—"

"Like hell it is. You just let me decide what's best for this family."

"Any dude ever comes in here and tries to hurt you again, Ma," Timmy said, "we wouldn't even have to blow him away. Just show him this, the sumbitch'd crap in his pants and run like a rabbit with a firecracker up his ass."

"Watch your mouth," I said automatically.

"Sure," he said, but he wasn't paying attention to me. His eyes, still wide and shiny, were all over the rifle. He moved to the table and ran his fingers over the short barrel, the long middle section, the pistol grip. "Wow," he said again.

"You're not going to keep this in here," I said to Jack. "I won't have it in the house."

"You don't have nothing to say about it. I've got a safe place all picked out."

"What safe place?"

"Never mind. You don't need to know."

"It won't be loaded?"

"Damn right it will."

"Each box magazine holds thirty rounds," Timmy said. "Bam, bam, bam, bam!"

"Jack . . ." My voice cracked a little, I couldn't help it. "You're not thinking of letting Timmy fire it?"

"Why not? He's old enough to learn."

"At *what*, for God's sake?"

"Same thing I'm going to practice on. Targets."

"But it's against the law—"

"Screw the law. The guy I bought it from knows another collector who owns a big ranch where you can shoot as many rounds as you want, no worries about the cops."

"Bam, bam, bam, bam," Timmy said again. "Bam bam bam bam!"

Jack didn't seem to notice the way Timmy kept touching the ugly gun, looking at it in that hot-eyed awestruck way. No, it was worse than just awestruck. It was unnatural, worshipful, almost . . . sexual. Oh my Lord! Ten years old and getting off on that thing. As if he were imagining firing it, cutting somebody in half with it.

It scared me. It made me as afraid as I'd been while I was being beaten and raped.

COURTNEY REEVES

J ASON WENT OUT AGAIN tonight and didn't come home until late
again. Real late. The bedside clock said it was almost two o'clock when
I heard him. I was still awake. I couldn't sleep when he stayed out late like
this. I kept worrying about where he'd gone, what he'd been doing.

Ladybug was curled up next to me. Jason doesn't like her sleeping on
the bed when we're together, but I let her come up when I'm alone. She's
a comfort, like the big floppy-eared teddy bear I'd had when I was a kid.
She started to whimper a little when she heard Jason. I put my hand
around her muzzle to keep her quiet. I didn't want him to know I'd been
lying awake worrying, so I'd pretend to be asleep when he came into the
bedroom.

But he didn't come in. I heard him doing something in the kitchen, not
being too quiet about it, then moving around in the living room, then
nothing at all. It got so quiet I could hear Ladybug's tummy rumbling.

I lay there waiting a long time, almost half an hour. Then I couldn't wait
anymore. I got up and put on my robe and slippers and went out into the
living room, shutting the bedroom door so Ladybug couldn't follow
me. Jason hadn't turned on any lights, but he had the TV going with the
sound muted. He was sitting there in the dark drinking a bottle of beer
and staring at some people shooting each other in black and white on
the screen.

"Jason?"

He hadn't heard me come in. He jerked forward on the couch, twisting around toward me. "Christ. What's the idea sneaking up like that?"

"I wasn't sneaking."

"You walk like a freakin' cat sometimes."

"I'm sorry. I couldn't sleep and I heard you out here—"

"Go back to bed."

"Why are you sitting in the dark with the TV on?"

"Because I feel like it, that's why."

There was enough flickery light from the screen so I could see him reach up and rub at his cheek and then grimace like he was in pain.

"What's the matter, honey?"

"Nothing's the matter." He took a long swallow of beer.

"It's after two. How come you were out so late?"

"Don't start ragging on me, goddamn it."

"I'm not ragging—"

"Go back to bed, leave me alone."

He sounded funny in a way that made my skin prickle and crawl. *Oh God,* I thought, *he's stoned. And not on weed.* "You promised me," I said.

"What?"

"You promised you wouldn't do that shit anymore."

"What shit? What the hell you talking about?"

"Go out partying, get cranked up."

"Who says I'm cranked up? Huh?" He reached up to rub his cheek again. "Go on, get outta here."

Instead I stepped over to the end table and switched on the lamp. I couldn't help doing it, I had to see him in the light. Oh! Oh! He was high on meth, all right, I could see it in his eyes and the way he was kind of shivering—that's one of the things about meth, it can make you feel chilled when you're starting to come down. But that wasn't all. He had a bruise on his cheekbone, a cut crusty with dried blood under his eye.

"Shut that fucking light off!"

I didn't; I went and sat down next to him—I couldn't help doing that, either. "Jason, what happened to your face? It looks like you were in a fight."

No answer. I leaned close, close enough to hear how fast his heart was beating. Too close. He shoved me away, hard enough so I almost fell off the couch. He glared at me, and then all of a sudden he threw the beer bottle at the TV. It just missed the screen, hit the stand instead, and spewed beer and foam all over the carpet. Then he got up and went around me and almost knocked the lamp off the table switching it off.

"Pooch," I said. "That son of a bitch Pooch."

". . . All right. Yeah, Pooch, so what? I felt like partying tonight. So what?"

I had a feeling in my stomach like I wanted to throw up. Pooch. Fat, ugly Pooch with his greasy ponytail and bad breath. Cooking and selling meth on that run-down farm of his across the river, getting girls hooked because it was the only way he could get one to go to bed with him. The one time I'd made the mistake of going over there with Jason and letting him talk me into trying some crystal, Pooch had tried to hit on me with his mouth and his blubbery hands. Pig!

"Is he the one you had the fight with?"

"I don't fight with my friends."

He's not your friend! But I didn't say it. I said, "Then who?"

Jason didn't answer at first and I thought he wasn't going to. But then he said, "Shouldn't sell to pricks that turn mean when they're cranked up."

"What prick?"

"Roy, that's what prick."

"Who's Roy?"

"You don't know him. Better believe I gave him worse than he gave me." Jason rubbed at the bruise again. "Why're you still here? Go to bed, no more talking tonight."

"Jason . . ."

"Go to bed!"

He stomped into the kitchen and opened the fridge and yanked out another beer. The light from inside made him look big and mean himself, not like Jason at all, like somebody I didn't know or want to know. I made myself walk slow to the bedroom door. Once I was inside, I had this crazy impulse to lock it. But if I did that and he wanted to come in, as messed up as he was, he might kick the door down. So I didn't.

Ladybug whimpered and licked my face when I got back into bed. She always knows when I'm feeling bad, and she tries to comfort me the best way she knows how. I hadn't felt this bad since I was raped. I couldn't feel much worse right now.

Jason hadn't just been partying with Pooch and whoever Roy was. There'd been girls there, too. Sex as well as meth. When I was close to him out there on the couch, I could smell it on him. He couldn't wait until I was ready to make love again, he just had to go screw somebody else. Be unfaithful, something I'd never do to him. For the first time?

I didn't want to know. Yes, I did. No, I didn't.

I hugged Ladybug tight, real tight, and cried myself to sleep.

GRIFFIN KELLS

Thursday morning, and we were still stymied. No witnesses, no leads, no suspects. It made me feel like a squirrel in a cage, running around and around and getting nowhere fast.

Robert and his IU team had finished working their way through the list of individuals who might have had a revenge motive for the Torrey homicide, and except for Jack Spivey, now eliminated, none of the interrogations had raised a red flag. I'd put Karl Simms in charge of interviewing members of the neighborhood watch patrols—groups of that sort have a vigilante mind-set, usually benign and law-abiding, sometimes not; they've been known to attract individuals angry enough and disturbed enough to take the law into their own hands. He hadn't come up with anything, either.

Little we could do now except go back over old ground and wait and hope and pray for a break.

ANGELA LOWENSTEIN

Tony wanted me to stay the night with him. He asked while we were walking across the Valley JC campus after the end of our Thursday-evening business admin class.

"I wish I could," I said, "but I can't. Not tonight."

"Why not?"

"Work at the *Clarion* tomorrow. I have to be there early."

"Why? The Friday edition will already be out."

"Daddy's request. There's some bookkeeping he needs me to do."

"You could drive up early in the morning."

"Uh-uh. I'd have to get up at the crack of dawn and go to my apartment first to put on clean clothes."

"Okay, then how about just coming to my place for an hour or so now?"

"Uh-uh to that, too. An hour with you always turns into two or more. And I'm tired and I need to get some sleep. If I go into the office looking bedraggled, Daddy's liable to guess why."

"Well, he must have some idea we've been sleeping together."

"I don't think so. He still thinks of me as his little girl. And he's kind of old-fashioned when it comes to sex."

"Good thing his daughter isn't."

"Hah," I said, and when I leaned up to kiss him, I yanked his ear.

We made a date for Saturday night. I could stay over at Tony's apartment then and spend most of Sunday with him. Sunday is Daddy's one day of rest; we have a pact that if I don't bother him then, he won't bother me.

It's a fifteen-mile drive up-valley from the college to Santa Rita, and Tony was on my mind the whole way. He wasn't the first guy I'd had sex with—Daddy would have a fit if he knew I was seventeen when I lost my virginity—but Tony was my first real love. I didn't have any doubts that he felt the same way about me. We were good together, in bed and in every other way. We liked the same things, we had the same opinions on politics and religion and gay rights and the environment, we made each other laugh, and we'd never had a serious argument much less a fight in the eight months we'd been together.

Daddy thought Tony was gearing up to ask me to marry him, but that wasn't going to happen. Tony wasn't keen on marriage. For that matter, neither was I. Not right now, anyway—not until I had my diploma and a job with a good CPA firm, maybe not until I'd had enough experience to establish my own business.

What Tony *had* asked me to do was to give up my apartment and move in with him. Or if not that, then move into a brand-new place together. Well, I was tempted. I'd said no, I wasn't ready for that kind of commitment, but the more I saw him and the more I missed him when we were apart, the more tempted I became. I was weakening and he knew it and kept bringing up the subject, usually after we'd just finished making love.

The problem was Daddy and his old-fashioned attitudes and expectations. If I did decide to take Tony up on his proposal, I dreaded telling Daddy. He could be stubborn and inflexible on certain subjects and "living in sin" was one of them. Funny in a way, because otherwise he was pretty liberal. Maybe it was because he'd had such a bad marriage to my mother—I hadn't seen her since they split up when I was seven, didn't even know if she was alive or dead—and he'd never come close to marrying again, hardly even dated. You'd think he was soured on the institution of marriage, but he wasn't. He still considered it the right and proper way for couples, straight, gay, or lesbian, to cohabit. A bundle of contradictions, that was Daddy.

So he'd raise holy hell with me if I moved in with Tony "without benefit of clergy," as he'd put it. I loved him a lot, and the last thing I wanted to do was hurt him, but I loved Tony, too, and you have to do what you feel is best for you and your future. When the time came to tell Daddy, and probably it'd be sooner than later, I'd just have to bite the bullet and endure his wrath. Then when he cooled down, I'd find ways to get back into his good graces. He liked Tony, they got along pretty well, and more than anything he wanted me to be happy. He'd come around eventually.

It was nearly eleven when I got to my apartment building on Northridge. It's a small place, eight units on two floors, and my apartment is just three rooms and a bath, but it was all I could afford right now. Daddy had grumbled about my moving out on my own, then raised my *Clarion* salary to help with the rent. Another of his contradictions. Tony's place in the valley was larger and nicer—his folks had money and he had a part-time job—and it would be more comfortable, not to mention more pleasurable, living there with him.

I smiled to myself. *You're weakening, all right, Angela,* I thought.

One thing you could say for this building was that it was well lit outside, so you didn't have to worry walking from the parking slots along the side to the front door. I let myself in, climbed the stairs to the second floor. Mrs. Sullivan in 2B had her TV on late and loud, as usual, some silly sitcom rerun with a laugh track. It was a good thing her apartment was at the far end from mine, so the TV noise didn't penetrate once I was inside. I keyed open my door, stepped through, closed the door behind me, and started to reach for the light switch.

Breathy sound. Movement, close by.

Somebody here, hiding in the dark!

A rush of disbelief and sudden panic made me swing around and fumble for the knob, get the door open, get away . . . too late. An arm caught me hard around the throat; a gloved hand slapped over my mouth and twisted my head around. A man's body pressed into mine from behind, pushed me up tight against the wall. Something sharp jabbed my cheek, trailed a line of fire down over my neck.

"You scream or try to fight me, I'll slit your fucking throat from ear to ear, you understand me, bitch!" Raspy voice, muffled, the words all run together.

No! No, no, no!

Confusion, raw terror, as he shoved me across the dark room, leathery fingers pinching my mouth shut, heavy breathing close to my ear like a dog panting. Where . . . ? The couch. He threw me down hard on the couch, facedown, rough cushion fabric scraping across my chin and cheek. His heavy weight came down on top of me, a knee jammed into the middle of my back. I felt a cut of pain behind my ear . . . the knife again.

"Lie still, don't move, don't make a sound, I'll kill you if you do."

He jerked his hand away from my mouth. Threw my coat up over my head. Yanked my skirt up. Clawed at my panties, ripped them off. Leathery fingers stroked and pinched my bare buttocks, the raspy voice whispering, "Nice ass, sweet ass, all mine now, baby, all mine, all mine."

The fingers stopped stroking and pinching.

Zipper sound.

No!

I moved a little then, I couldn't help it. He hit me with his fist, the pain strangling a cry in my throat. Another blow made my ears ring. Worms of blood crawled on my skin.

"I told you to lie still, keep quiet!" The knife jabbed me again. "Cut your throat from ear to ear, you hear me, ear to ear."

Rubbery sliding sound. Condom. Putting on a condom.

More panting, then an excited giggling as he spread my butt cheeks apart. "Now you get what you got coming, you stuck-up bitch, now you get it good!"

I bit into the cushion, cringing, holding my breath, waiting for the terrible new pain when he forced himself inside and began raping me. And all I could think was *Please don't kill me.*

Please please please don't kill me!

PART THREE

FRIDAY, APRIL 22

ROBERT ORTIZ

SOFIA AND I WERE making love when the call came from night sergeant Sam Mitchum. Such grim irony. A gentle act of love interrupted by word of another savage act of hate.

I switched on the bedside lamp, swung naked from bed while I continued to listen and speak briefly to Mitchum.

"What is it?" Sofia asked when I ended the conversation. "What's happened?"

"Another woman was attacked tonight." Anger burned hot in me again; I had to make an effort to keep my voice even. "Ted Lowenstein's daughter, in her apartment."

"*Madre de Dios!*" She made the sign of the cross. "That poor girl. Is she badly hurt?"

"She's alive and was able to make a nine-one-one call."

"Roberto . . . the same evil one?"

I shook my head without answering. What could I say? It was too soon, the initial information too sparse.

Sofia watched me finish hurriedly dressing, saying nothing more. But we knew each other so well—the same thoughts were in her mind as in mine. I had been so certain, with Martin Torrey dead, that there would be no more assaults. Now this, a fifth that seemed to follow the same general MO as the others. It sickened as well as infuriated me to think that I could have been so wrong. That the serial might still be at large.

That women remained in jeopardy and Angela Lowenstein might not be the last victim.

Her father had been informed, as had Chief Kells and Captain Judkins, and calls had gone out to the other IU officers. As with the previous victims, she would be taken to the hospital ER for examination and treatment. Susan Sinclair was on her way to Santa Rita General. Al Bennett, Joe Bloom, and Karl Simms would meet me at the crime scene.

With the aid of siren and red light, I reached the Northridge Street address in less than twenty minutes. An EMT unit, an ambulance, and two black-and-whites were there, all with their flashers staining the night. The patrolmen had already put up CRIME SCENE signs. Al Bennett, who lived not far from Northridge, had already arrived as well and must be inside with the EMTs, since neither he nor any of them were in sight. As late as it was, after midnight, a crowd had gathered and was being controlled by three of the uniforms; a fourth officer, Leo Malatesta, stood in conversation with a cluster of men and women in bathrobes I assumed were neighbors.

I wedged my cruiser in next to Al's, called to Malatesta as I headed toward the open front door of the building, "Which apartment?"

"Three B, second floor," he called back. "EMTs just took a gurney up."

Inside, I hurried up the stairs. Al was in the hallway outside 3B. The entryway was blocked by the gurney and the EMTs, who were tending to the victim. I could see that her head, face, and neck were battered and bloody, her mouth twisted into a frozen grimace, her eyes open and staring.

Al drew me aside, his dark face drawn tight. "Bastard really did a job on her. Sodomized, cut, beaten, same as the other four."

"Was she able to say anything about the perp?"

"Masked, wore gloves, had a knife. Waiting inside when she got home. That's all we could get out of her."

"Wait here. I'll be back after they bring her out."

I went downstairs again to talk to Malatesta. None of the neighbors he'd spoken to had anything to tell. There had been no screams or other loud noises from the victim's apartment, the perp had not been seen leaving the premises. The first anyone had known of the assault was when the response units began arriving with flashers and sirens.

Murmurs and stirrings came from the onlookers—the EMTs had appeared with the gurney. Angela Lowenstein lay prone under a blanket, her head turned in my direction, the one visible eye still staring glassily. A few of the watchers strained forward for a better look, their faces tinged a hellish red by the flasher lights.

"Damn ghouls," Malatesta muttered.

The EMTs made quick work of loading the gurney into the ambulance. Just as it pulled away, siren wailing, Karl Simms drove up. I supplied a brief rundown of the situation, then sent him and Malatesta to hunt up any neighbors not already interviewed.

No sooner had this been done than Joe Bloom arrived. He hauled his evidence bag out of the backseat, saw me, and hurried over.

"Bad," he said on the way upstairs. "As bad as it gets. Ted Lowenstein's daughter, for God's sake. Does he know yet?"

"Yes."

"Poor guy. I wouldn't want to be in his shoes."

I thought of Valentina and Daniela. So young, so vulnerable. *Dios los protege contra daño.* A similar prayer by Ted Lowenstein for the safety of his daughter had gone unanswered. I knew exactly what he must be feeling, the anguish and the sadness, the impotent rage.

Al Bennett was still in the hallway standing guard. "Watch out for the blood on the carpet there," he said, pointing, as he led the way inside the apartment.

The assault had taken place in the living room, on a couch along the right-hand wall. The couch and an end table had been pulled askew; one plaid cushion was tilted down onto the carpet. Streaks and spatters of blood stained it, the other cushions, and one padded arm. The blood on the carpet formed a spotted trail leading to where a maroon leather handbag lay overturned near the door, its contents strewn about. A larger amount of blood had collected at that point.

"Perp must've knocked the purse out of her hand when he grabbed her," Al said. "Then after he was finished with her, she crawled off the couch and over here to get her cell phone. She was lying there with it in her hand when the EMTs came."

"How did he get inside?" I asked.

"That's the question. Far as I could tell, he didn't break in."

I checked the lock on the front door. Confirmed. A dead bolt that bore no marks of forcible entry. From there I stepped carefully around the blood trail and went to look in the other rooms. The three windows— one each in the living room, bedroom, and bathroom—were all locked, their latches likewise free of force marks.

Nothing seemed to have been disturbed in any of those rooms or in the kitchenette. A small teakwood jewelry box sat on the bedroom dresser; I nudged it open with a knuckle. It contained earrings, bracelets, pendants on thin silver chains. None of the items appeared to be particularly valuable, but most would be worth enough to tempt anyone intent on theft.

I returned to the living room. Joe was taking digital evidence pictures, both video and close-up stills. He had put on surgical gloves and I asked him to check through the wallet that had been dumped out of the purse. Twenty-six dollars in cash, Visa card, Discover card, driver's license, several photographs in a glassine folder.

"The perp didn't steal anything," I said. "Or go into any of the other rooms, from the look of them."

"Only one thing on his sick mind," Joe said, "same as the other times."

Al said, "I've been thinking. He could've used a skeleton key to get in. The door lock's old, not all that secure."

Skeleton keys are not that easy to come by. Still, it was a possibility and I said as much.

"Here's another," he said. "Maybe she forgot to lock the door the last time she went out."

"Not likely. No intelligent woman living alone would make that kind of mistake."

"Well, she sure as hell didn't invite him in."

We were wasting time and energy in idle conjecture. I sent Al down to see how Karl was making out, then did what I could to assist Joe, who was now taking blood samples from the couch and carpet.

"Chances are it'll all turn out to be hers," he said. "Too much to hope for that she managed to spill some of his."

When he finished that task, he began hunting for trace evidence. After a time he said, "Got something here that didn't turn up at any of the other crime scenes. Pubic hair." He showed it to me before putting it into a glassine envelope with his tweezers. "Could be from her, could be from him. If it's his, a DNA match will nail him but good, once he's ID'd and apprehended." Joe added gloomily, "If he ever is."

TED LOWENSTEIN

I HAD BEEN AT the hospital for nearly three hours before I was told the extent of Angela's injuries and they let me see her. Until then all anybody would say was that she was being evaluated, tested, and treated, and that her condition was stable.

Evaluated. Tested. Treated.

Dear sweet Jesus.

I spent most of the time pacing the waiting room. I couldn't sit still for more than a minute or two. When I was first told I might have a long wait, I went outside and called Chief Kells. He had nothing to tell me yet. I asked him to do what he could to keep the out-of-town media wolves away from Angela and from me; he said he would try. Then I woke up Tyler James at home, told him tersely what had happened, informed him he would be in charge of operations for the next few days, and made the same request of him as I had of Chief Kells. When Tyler began expressing the usual sympathies, I broke the connection. I couldn't stand to listen to pointless, if well-meant, empathy. I would have to endure enough of it in the coming days, from all sorts of people, some of it genuine and some, from the likes of Mayor Delahunt and his cronies, insincere pro forma bullshit.

I paced and waited and watched the time crawl, making a conscious effort all the while not to think about what Angela had endured. Whenever I let the black imaginings slip through, fury would well up and I would have to fight off the urge to smash something. I am not a violent man, but if the inhuman piece of garbage who'd harmed Angela had been within my grasp, I would not have been able to control myself—I would have hurt him worse than he'd hurt her, I might even have tried to kill him.

After a while a kind of mental numbness set in, dulling the pain, holding the fury at bay. Now and then I checked my cell for voice mail messages. There were none. The rapist had apparently gotten away free again. Caution: monster at large.

Finally, *finally*, a doctor came in and put an end to the waiting. I knew him slightly; his name was Ferguson. Not an ER physician, one of the senior staff physicians—a middle-aged, gray-haired man with a thin mouth that looked as if it seldom smiled.

"Your daughter's condition remains stable, Mr. Lowenstein. She is doing as well as can be expected under the circumstances."

"'Doing as well as can be expected.' What does that mean, exactly?"

"Her injuries are not life threatening."

"What injuries, exactly? How serious?"

"Are you sure you want the specifics?"

"Yes. Everything. In layman's terms."

"Very well. She is suffering from shock, of course—that is to be expected in cases of severe trauma. There is considerable rectal tearing, and contusions and lacerations to the head and neck. Fortunately, none of the blows responsible resulted in either a fracture or a hematoma. Four relatively shallow cuts of various dimensions on the neck and upper back, two more on the right buttock, none requiring stitches."

The fury had returned as he spoke, a surge of it that set my temples to pounding. "The rectal damage . . . it's not permanent?"

"I wouldn't think so, no. Surgery is not indicated at this time."

"At this time. Meaning it may still be necessary?"

"Only if there are unexpected complications."

Unexpected complications. Staph infection, an ever-present danger in hospitals these days. God knew what else he meant.

"Where is she? I want to see her."

"ICU, a private room. She's under sedation. You won't be able to speak to her for several hours—"

"I want to see my daughter *now*," I said sharply this time.

"I'll allow it, but only briefly." He paused. "Before I summon a nurse, there's something else you should know. Your daughter was coherent enough when she was brought in to refuse a forensic medical examination."

"Refused it? Why?"

"She didn't give a reason. Nor is she required to. Refusal is her prerogative by law."

I knew that. But why would she say no? Some victims do, it's true; Eileen Jordan, the grade-school teacher, had also refused. Humiliated enough already, she'd said. Maybe that was Angela's reason. Or maybe it was because only the first of the rape kits taken in the other assaults had been processed—lack of funds, lack of initiative, the same old goddamn story—and had yielded no DNA, no physical evidence transferred onto the victim at the scene. Angela knew that; I'd written an editorial about the backup and slow processing of rape kits statewide . . .

The nurse who showed me to Angela's room reiterated Ferguson's instructions: maximum stay of three minutes, view but don't touch the patient. I had myself girded before we went in, but it nonetheless felt like being struck a physical blow. One of a loving father's worst nightmares, knowing what had been done to his daughter and seeing her like this.

She lay flat on her stomach, the visible side of her face chalky and scrunched up, one hand touching her chin—the kind of sleeping pose she'd favored as a child. IV tube taped to one arm. Bandage on her temple, another on her neck partially visible beneath the drawn-up covers. Swelling bruise on her cheekbone.

The fury simmered, threatened to take over again; I battled it down. Took a step toward the bed, but the nurse laid a restraining hand on my arm and I stood still again. The constriction in my chest made it difficult to breathe. I had never felt more helpless in my life.

I made no effort to stay in the room more than the allotted time. Three minutes was all I could bear right now; later, when she was awake, when I'd had more time to clamp a lid on my emotions, it would be a little easier to look at her in that bed with my eyes dry and my vision clear.

GRIFFIN KELLS

IT WAS EARLY MORNING before Susan Sinclair called from the hospital to report that Angela Lowenstein was well enough to be interrogated.

She also reported that a forensic medical exam had been refused. No reason given by the victim, but she had been made aware of what it entailed; Susan thought that the necessity of providing a complete and thorough medical and sexual history, as well as being subjected to a full-body physical examination, was the reason the girl had balked. Sexually active young women are not always comfortable discussing their private lives with strangers, especially when they have a father as doting and straitlaced as Ted Lowenstein. The refusal was of no real consequence, given the backlog of rape-kit testing and the unlikelihood of one revealing anything useful.

I had been at the station all night and I was dog tired. A couple of hours of sleep on the sofa in my office hadn't done much except make me feel logy and short-tempered; a shower and a shave and half a pot of coffee hadn't helped any, either. The lack yet again of leads in this fifth assault and its probable repercussions were a heavy weight.

Calls had begun to pour in to the police lines and my cell as word spread. The only ones I deemed necessary to deal with immediately were from Ted Lowenstein, Frank Judkins, District Attorney Gavin Conrad, Councilman Hitchens, and Mayor Delahunt. The mayor was full of outrage, moral indignation, and his usual criticism of me and my department's methods; he demanded I meet with him in his office at eleven o'clock, implying without saying so that others would be present. Pendergast and Young, probably. An adversarial meeting, in any event. I told him tersely I'd be there unless police business intervened and cut him off.

Lieutenant Ortiz had conducted the four previous interrogations, but I felt that I ought to handle this one because of my personal acquaintance with the victim. I had always gotten along well with Angela, as I had with her father, and I believed I had her trust; she might be more comfortable with me asking intimate questions than Robert, who tended to be blunt. Also, if she was able to tell us anything that required immediate action, I would be right there to set the wheels in motion.

Robert and I left the station together but drove to the hospital in separate vehicles. Susan, in uniform, her short graying hair finger-rumpled, was waiting outside Angela's private room. She is a highly competent officer, compassionate in her role of victims' advocate, but with an otherwise no-nonsense attitude learned from her father and grandfather, both of whom were retired policemen. Ted Lowenstein was with his daughter now, she told us before we entered.

It wasn't easy, walking in on them. Angela's battered condition was gut-wrenching because of the personal connection. She lay half over on her left side in the elevated bed, in obvious discomfort, but her eyes were clear except for flickers of pain. Her father sat beside her, holding her hand, unshaven and gaunt from his all-night vigil. For the first time since I'd known him he wore a jacket, an old brown corduroy with patched elbows, and a white dress shirt instead of one of his trademark Hawaiian shirts. He wanted to stay during the questioning, but Angela said, "No, Daddy, no, please," and I asked him to leave. The room was already crowded and it wouldn't have done him any good to hear the details of the assault.

When he left, I sat in the chair he'd occupied and told Angela how sorry I was. Ghost of a smile in response. Susan pulled the only other chair over alongside me and set up the portable recorder. Robert went to stand against the wall next to the door to observe and listen.

Susan began the interrogation by saying, "If any questions make you feel uncomfortable, Angela, you don't have to give specific answers. But as we discussed before, the more information you can provide, the better."

"I'll tell everything I can remember." Small voice, but steady.

I said, keeping my tone gentle, "The man was waiting in your apartment when you arrived home, is that right?"

"In the dark, yes. He grabbed me before I could turn on the lights."

"The door was securely locked?"

"Yes. I never leave it unlocked."

"Do you have any idea how he got in?"

"No."

"Does anyone besides you have a key?"

"No. Well, Tony did."

"Tony?"

"My boyfriend. Tony Ciccoti. He lives in Riverton." Angela's lips trembled; she caught the lower one between her teeth. "You called him, didn't you?" she asked Susan.

"Of course. He should be here by now."

"He must have been upset . . . wasn't he?"

"More than upset and very concerned. You can see him after we're done here."

The answer seemed to relieve Angela. As though she'd been afraid he might not want to come, might somehow blame her for the attack—a typical victim response. She must really care for him, to need him as much as she needed her father.

"About your apartment key, Angela. You said Tony *did* have one. Meaning he doesn't any longer?"

"No. I had to ask for it back."

"Why?"

"I lost mine."

"Oh? When was that?"

"A couple of weeks ago."

"Do you know where you lost it?"

"No. It must have fallen out of my purse. I couldn't find it anywhere."

"Only the apartment key, or others as well?"

"Only that one. I kept it separate, on a small dream catcher."

Dream catcher. Native American object decorated with beads and feathers that is supposed to filter out bad dreams, ward off evil spirits.

"Was there anything else attached to the key or on the key itself with the address of your building?"

"No. Just the key and the dream catcher."

"Do you always keep your purse with you?"

"Yes."

"Never leave it unattended for any reason?"

"Unattended?"

"Where someone might have access to it."

"You mean my key could've been stolen? No. I wouldn't . . . no."

I let a few seconds pass before I asked, "Have you noticed anyone hanging around your apartment building, a man who doesn't live there?"

"No."

"Someone following or watching you, in a car or on foot?"

"Stalking me?" Angela was silent for several seconds, working her memory. Then: "No. Nobody like that."

"Have you received any anonymous phone calls, cell or landline?"

"You mean . . . obscene? No."

"A caller hanging up when you answer?"

"No."

"Has a man made advances to you recently?"

". . . Sexual advances? No."

"Not necessarily sexual," I said. "Asked you for a date and became angry or aggressive when you rejected him."

"I get asked sometimes, but . . . no, nothing like that. Why? You don't think the man might be somebody I know?"

"We have to look at all the possibilities."

"Yes, but . . . He's the same one who raped those other women, isn't he? What he did to me . . . he must be the same man. A stranger . . . picked me at random like the others . . ."

She was becoming agitated, fright and confusion like a shadow play on her pale, bruised face. Susan calmed her with a gentle touch and a few murmured words.

"Are you up to talking about the assault now?" I asked.

". . . Yes."

"You said the assailant grabbed you before you could turn on the lights."

"I heard him breathing and I tried to get away, but he . . . his arm was around my neck and his hand over my mouth. Then he pushed me up against the wall and stuck . . . stuck me with the knife."

"So you didn't get a clear look at him at any time during the attack."

"No. It all happened in the dark."

"Can you estimate his size? Tall or short, thin or fat?"

"Not much taller than me . . . not fat . . ."

Average. Same description as in the previous four cases.

"His age? Twenties, thirties, forties?"

"Not forties . . ." Angela hesitated, working her memory again. "Young, but not very young . . . not a teenager."

"A man under thirty."

"I . . . think so."

That was something different. Maybe. The consensus among the other victims was that the perp had been older, thirties, possibly forty. Angela could be misestimating his age; traumatic experiences can blur and distort specific details.

"What did he say to you?"

"He said . . . he said if I screamed he'd slit my throat."

"Was his voice familiar?"

". . . It was muffled . . . the mask."

"But it might have been familiar? Do you have that impression?"

"I don't know . . . maybe, but I can't be sure."

"Was there anything distinctive about it?"

"Raspy. A fast, raspy whisper."

"Fast?"

"His words . . . he ran them all together."

"What else did he say?"

"Nothing until after he dragged me over to the couch—" She broke off, shifting position, the pain flickers in her eyes again. "Straight to the couch, in the dark. He must've been there for a while."

"Why do you say that?"

"There's usually a chair between the couch and the door. He must've moved it out of the way."

Susan said, "Either he put the lights on to look around or he had a flashlight. Making preparations while he waited."

Which implied that he'd had some kind of advance notice that she wouldn't be home and when to expect her back. Stalking her whether he was known to her or not.

"He threw me down on the couch," Angela said, "fell on top of me with his knee in my back. He said if I moved or made a sound he'd kill me. Then he . . . then . . . he kept hitting me, panting like an animal, like a dog, and I heard him . . . he . . ."

Her eyes were squeezed shut, the anguish again audible in her voice.

Susan said, "It's not necessary for you to go into any more detail." But Angela didn't seem to hear her. "Giggling the whole time he was doing it . . . but thank God it didn't last long, he didn't last long . . . I thought he was going to kill me when he was done, but all he did was tell me not to scream or he'd come back and . . . fuck me again, and then he was gone and I . . . I . . ."

Reliving the ordeal was too much for her. She buried her face in the pillow, her body shaking with smothered sobs.

Susan stood up, saying, "That's all for now, no more questions," the words directed to me as much as to Angela, then reached for the bell to summon a nurse.

Robert and I got out of there as soon as the nurse arrived. My mouth was dry and there was a hard knot in my throat that made it difficult to swallow. You get hardened to victim interrogations along with everything else in police work, but now and then emotions seep through the shell and you're not quite able to dam up the leaks.

Ted Lowenstein was waiting with Angela's boyfriend, Tony Ciccoti, a good-looking young man with a mop of shaggy black hair. The anger and anxiety they were feeling was palpable. Ted asked if she had been able to tell us anything that would help identify her assailant, if it was the same man who had committed the previous assaults. I hedged by giving the same answer to both questions: too soon to tell. Which was the truth, but not what he or the boyfriend wanted to hear.

Susan and the nurse came out of Angela's room. Angela was asking for Tony; Susan took him in to her.

"Christ, Chief," Ted said to me, "you've got to nail the bastard this time. You've *got* to, you hear? You've got to!"

It's foolish to make premature vows in police work, but I made one anyway—for my temporary peace of mind as well as for Lowenstein's. "We will," I said, thinking, *This time, by God, we'd better.*

HOLLY DEXTER

Nick and I heard about it at breakfast. He likes to listen to the news on the local radio station while he's eating, God knows why, as depressing as it usually is. But this morning I was glad he did.

Well, *glad* isn't the right word. It was a shock, really, and I didn't know how I should feel. I mean, I had all sorts of conflicting emotions. I was sorry for the poor Lowenstein girl, and outraged and nervous again because women in Santa Rita were still at risk, but at the same time I felt relieved—mainly for Liane, but for myself, too. I never believed for a minute, any more than she had, that Marty was the rapist, and now we had proof of it. Proof that his murder was utterly senseless. I hoped to God the crazy person who'd shot him was feeling sick now over the mistake he'd made, maybe even sick enough to turn himself in to the police.

I said that to Nick as I got up from the table, and he said, "Don't bet on it. He probably still thinks he was justified."

"Why would he think that, after what just happened?"

"Took a sex offender off the streets, didn't he?"

I glared at him. "For God's sake, how can you say that? Marty never hurt anybody. And he paid for what he did in Ohio, paid and paid—"

"I didn't say that's how I feel, I said that's how the guy who pulled the trigger might feel."

"The cops better catch him."

"Chances are they won't," Nick said. "They still haven't caught the rapist, have they?"

Great. Terrific. Mr. Optimist.

I went to call Liane and tell her the news if she hadn't heard yet. But there was no answer on her cell or her landline. That added worry to the rest of what I was feeling. She should be home at this hour, it was only a couple of minutes past eight o'clock. Well, maybe she'd changed her mind about going back to work right away. Zacks' Dental Care opened for business at eight. I called, but the woman who answered said no, Liane wasn't there and wasn't expected. Allan was busy with a patient so I couldn't talk to him.

"I can't get hold of Liane," I said to Nick. "I'll drop you off at work and go try to find her."

He doesn't like me to drive his pickup, he says I grind the gears when I shift, but he didn't put up an argument. Good thing he didn't because I was in no mood for his whiny complaints. All he said was, "She's probably home. Just not taking calls."

"Well, maybe, but does she know about the new rape yet or not, that's the question. I hope she doesn't. I should be the one to break it to her."

"Uh-huh."

I couldn't tell if he was being snotty or not, so I just let it pass.

He insisted on driving to the brewery, and when we got there, he told me before he got out to be careful not to grind the gears. I ground them deliberately when I left him standing at the main gate. Damn the gears! As if they were important at a time like this.

I rang the bell when I got to the Grove Street house, but the door stayed shut. I used my key and went all through the house. Liane wasn't there. And my car wasn't in the garage or anywhere on the street.

Now I was really worried. Where could she have gone so early in the day?

HUGH DELAHUNT

THERE WERE SEVEN OF us at table in the conference room. In addition to me: Craig, Frank Judkins, Vernon Nichols (there to take notes), and three members of the city council, Evan Pendergast, Aretha Young, and Oliver Bonnard. I had arranged the meeting for ten thirty, to give us time for discussion before Chief Kells arrived at eleven. If he arrived on time.

Heaven knows I take no pleasure in the misfortune of others, even those who have, for no supportable reasons, declared themselves my enemy, but if another poor woman had to be raped in Santa Rita, I could hardly be unhappy that it was Angela Lowenstein. I had nothing against the girl, although she had been as unpleasant to me on occasion as her father always was. Naturally I was appalled by what had been done to her, and as concerned for her well-being as I had been for that of the other rape victims. But I would be less than honest if I didn't admit that the assault had its beneficial aspects where my interests were concerned.

Lowenstein would be too preoccupied for quite a while to continue his badgering tactics, and by the time he resumed, if and when he did, they would no longer have much impact. And if Kells and Ortiz continued to fail at catching the rapist, Lowenstein would surely be disinclined to continue his support of them. But it wouldn't do for me to wait for further proof of their incompetence. The time to begin strongly lobbying for Kells's dismissal was now, while matters were in flux.

"You all know why I called this meeting," I began. "Another vicious rape, this time the daughter of a fairly prominent citizen. Until now we all believed, or at least fervently hoped, that these atrocities had ended with the death of Martin Torrey. Obviously that is not the case. The maniac responsible, whoever he is, continues to pose a grave threat. He *must* be stopped, and quickly."

I paused for a moment while heads nodded in agreement. Then I said to Judkins, "Frank, has any progress been made as yet?"

"As far as I'm aware, no."

"As far as you're aware? Surely Chief Kells and Lieutenant Ortiz keep you informed."

"Usually."

"Usually?"

"When they have something important to discuss."

"Only then? No strategy meetings or the like?"

"Sometimes."

"You outrank Lieutenant Ortiz. Yet Chief Kells seems to have given him carte blanche in these investigations."

"Well, not quite. Ortiz is in charge of the IU, and my duties are mainly administrative."

"Nevertheless. Do you consider him a competent investigator?"

"He's well trained and has a good record."

"That isn't what I asked. Is he competent?"

Frank ran a hand over his liver-spotted pate, then adjusted his tie. He, at least, wore his uniform regularly, as befitted a ranking police officer— another point in his favor as Kells's replacement. "Seems to be. Most of the time."

"Have you spoken to him or to Chief Kells today?"

"Both of them, briefly. They had nothing definite to report."

"Which means, then, that once again they're completely stymied."

"Well, for the time being, anyway. There were no evident leads at the crime scene, but it's early yet. Something may develop."

"Something may develop," Evan Pendergast repeated. His chair creaked as he shifted his nearly three-hundred-pound bulk. "We've heard that for almost five months now. What about the Torrey murder? Has anything developed yet on that?"

"No."

"So we have five months of investigation into five brutal rapes and a homicide, and nothing worthwhile has come to light."

Aretha Young cleared her throat. She was a middle-aged, feisty black woman whose support I had cultivated when I first ran for mayor. The more minorities in my camp, the better. For their cause, too, of course. "Suppose you were in charge, Captain," she said. "Would you have handled the investigations any differently than Kells and Ortiz have?"

"There are some things I'd have done differently, yes."

"Such as?"

"Called in more outside help, for one thing. Not just from the DA and sheriff's department—from the attorney general, the FBI."

"FBI?" Oliver Bonnard said. "These rapes aren't federal crimes."

"No, but the FBI will sometimes provide assistance on such cases."

"Requesting help from the Bureau was suggested to Chief Kells. He told us the FBI seldom becomes involved in such matters, and then when they do, it's at their instigation."

"Not always at their instigation," Frank said. "A request for assistance can be made to the Justice Department."

"Aren't such requests usually declined?"

"Well, yes, but again, not always."

"Chief Kells believes that bringing in more outsiders would create jurisdictional problems. You don't agree?"

"No. I believe I could prevent that from happening."

"Captain Judkins is much more diplomatic than Chief Kells," Craig chimed in. Every now and then he surprises me by making a worthwhile contribution.

"And considerably more experienced in police work," I said. I ran a forefinger over my mustache. The hairs were so fine they had an almost silky feel, which my wife, Margaret, had remarked upon more than once in an intimate moment. "You'd have given the outside investigators more time, more latitude—in other words, taken full advantage of their expertise?"

"I would have, yes."

"And you believe that with their help the rapist would have been identified and arrested by now?" Bonnard asked.

"I do."

"In which event," I added, "the tragic death of Martin Torrey, a less than stellar but innocent individual, would have been prevented."

Bonnard nodded. He had been a Kells supporter all along, but that was because he invariably sided with the majority in any council decision. He was a fence-straddler by nature, and I was fairly sure he could be pushed over to our side, which was why I had invited him. All we would need then was one more vote, and with continued failure by Kells and Ortiz and sufficient pressure, we'd get it.

"It is my considered opinion," I said, "that it's time, past time, to make a leadership change in the Santa Rita Police Department. Are we all in agreement on that?"

"I don't know," Bonnard said, "it seems a little premature to me." Still fence-straddling. But not for long.

Evan said, "Premature? Five months, man. Five months and no end in sight with Kells in charge!"

"I meant premature because the attack on Ted Lowenstein's daughter happened only last night. I'd like to hear what Kells has to say about it, what he's doing and what he intends to do."

"So would we all," I said. "And we soon will, if he arrives on schedule. But I doubt he'll have anything to tell us that will change our minds about his lack of competence."

He didn't. I would have been amazed if he had.

He was ten minutes late. He presented an even more undignified presence than usual—his suit looked as if he had slept in it, which he probably had—and he answered our questions with an uncharacteristic snippiness. All of that, plus his steadfast refusal to call in outside assistance "except as a last resort," made a poor impression. Very poor, indeed.

Bonnard was off the fence and on my side by the time Kells left the conference room.

All it would take to convince one more council member to vote for Kells's dismissal was a few more days of ineffectual police work. I was convinced of that by the time the meeting ended. Just a few more days.

LIANE TORREY

I COULDN'T STAY COOPED up in the house after Allan called to tell me the news. I'd just ended the brief conversation with him when my cell rang again, then the landline right after that. Holly. She knew now, too, and she'd insist on coming over, on talking and talking about what had happened last night and what it meant, and I wasn't ready for that. She meant well and I loved her, but I didn't want to see her this morning. Or Allan or anybody else. I wanted to be alone for a while in some other place, somewhere empty of people, to try to sort out my feelings.

Before I left, I parted the curtains in the front window. There was no sign of any reporters yet, but they'd be around soon enough, ringing the bell, knocking on the door—another reason not to hang around here. I locked up and backed Holly's Subaru out of the garage and drove away quickly.

South of downtown, I turned inland on the county road that leads into the foothills to the east. There are several of them in long, rising folds with narrow little valleys tucked in between, the grass still bright green and studded with wildflowers, the live oaks and madrones and other trees in thickening copses the higher and farther I went. Hardly any traffic up here, and only scattered homes and ranches.

For a while, when the road crested a hill, I had glimpses of the winding course of the river in the distance. But then, as I climbed higher, I could no longer see it from any elevation. I preferred it that way. There was something about the river that I didn't like—a barren quality despite the trees and farms it serviced, a muddy-brown loneliness.

The road dropped down into a valley somewhat broader than the previous ones. Rolling meadows stretched away on both sides, bright with wild mustard and purple lupine, an intermingling of cattle and sheep grazing in little clusters. Halfway across, I pulled off onto the verge. A narrow stream ran between the road and the livestock fence here, stands of live oak hemming a section of open grassy bank that looked out over the meadow. A great many live oaks in these hills have succumbed and are still succumbing to sudden oak death, but these were a healthy-looking dusty green. A good place to sit and think, this—no cars, no people, no houses in sight. Quiet. Peaceful.

I went to perch on a mossy log next to the stream. A fair amount of winter-snow runoff flowed between its low banks. I watched the swift-moving water form little pools here and there, shallow and clear so that you could see the rocks and moss under the surface. And after a while my thoughts settled, grew as clear as the stream.

Another woman assaulted in the same way as the others, by the same man. I was sorry for that, but it was the kind of sorry you feel for any innocent stranger who has been badly abused, without strong emotional involvement. And there should have been because it meant that Martin was innocent, just as I had believed him to be; that now his memory would no longer be tainted by false accusations, false suspicion, and if the police finally did find out who had needlessly murdered him, his soul could rest in some measure of peace. This gave me a sense of vindication, satisfaction, imminent closure, yet those emotions were not as intense as they should have been. No matter how hard I tried, I couldn't make myself care as much as I should have.

Weary, worn-out, scooped out . . . that was part of the reason, yes. But there was more to it than that. I had grieved, but I hadn't been ravaged by grief. I had loved, but the love had grown tepid, and now it wasn't even that, it was cold. As cold as what had been left of Martin before they put him into the crematory oven.

What I was mostly feeling right now was a deep melancholy. I told myself that was only natural, that one day it would pass and I would regain my emotional equilibrium. I found a small stone in the grass and tossed it into one of the little pools, watched the ripples form and spread and then fade until the water was still and clear and peaceful again. Like that. Ripples that were soon enough gone, to be replaced once more by calm and clarity and peace.

Let me have that much, I thought. *Please. Let calm and clarity and peace be my legacy.*

The thought, unbidden, was almost like a prayer. But not to God, who could answer it.

To Martin James Torrey, who couldn't.

GRIFFIN KELLS

D AMN DELAHUNT AND HIS lynch mob.

That was exactly what the gathering had been, a politically moti-vated lynch mob with the noose in Delahunt's hands. Get rid of Griffin Kells, install yes-man Frank Judkins in his place. Run the police department the way he ran the city, the way he would run the county and then the state if he managed to get that far up the ladder.

He'd been after me from the beginning. If it hadn't been for the unwavering support of Dale Hitchens and the other three council members, and Ted Lowenstein and the *Clarion*, Delahunt would have had his way by now. Still would, after last night's fifth attack, unless we put the perp or perps behind bars in a hell of a hurry. Not even apprehending Martin Torrey's murderer would be enough to save my job, and Robert's. It had to be a definite end to the assaults.

There had been a time, between the third and fourth rapes, I'd considered resigning. My men and I hadn't been able to accomplish our sworn duty despite every effort; maybe somebody else in charge could. But Jenna had helped talk me out of it. My replacement would have been Captain Judkins then, as now—Delahunt would have seen to that—and Frank was no more qualified to head up this kind of investigation than I was. Less. Considerably less.

I'm a lot of things, but incompetent isn't one of them.

Delahunt might succeed in making me the scapegoat and getting rid of me, but I wouldn't go quietly. No pompous, self-promoting, mean-spirited politician was going to get away with impugning my dedication and my integrity, with leaving an undeserved black mark on my record and jeopardizing my future in law enforcement. I'd tell him and his cronies what I thought of them before I left Santa Rita, to their faces and in no uncertain terms. And then make sure Ted Lowenstein and other media outlets quoted me verbatim.

Hang me, Mayor?

Hang you!

EILEEN JORDAN

"YOU HAVEN'T HEARD?" BARBARA said. "Well, I hate to be the bearer of bad news . . ." Which she proceeded to bear, as people always do after that sort of preface.

I was not surprised. I had no reaction at all to the invader having claimed another victim. She might have called to discuss the weather or some other innocuous subject.

"That poor young woman. Isn't it awful, Eileen?"

"Yes, awful." But my response was automatic. I should have felt something—compassion, anger, something—but I felt nothing. It was as if all my emotions had withered away, and what remained were no more than dim impressions.

Shadows. Nothing left but shadows.

". . . some company?"

"I'm sorry, Barbara. What did you say?"

"I asked if you'd like some company. We could go out, have lunch, spend the day together—"

"Thank you, no. Not today."

"Forgive me for saying this, but you really should start living normally again. It isn't healthy to stay cooped up alone all the time."

Living normally. Meaningless phrase. What is normal? Is there such a state for a whole person, much less a shadow?

"Yes," I said, "you're right. But I'm just not feeling very well at the moment."

"Oh, of course—the shock. Why can't the police catch that maniac? My Lord, it has been nearly five months and they don't seem to have a clue who he is."

"No, apparently not."

There was a pause, indicating she was at a loss for anything else to say. I remained silent so as not to encourage her.

"Well," she said at length, "are you *sure* you don't want me to stop over, just for a little while?"

"I'd rather you didn't."

"Sometime soon, then. I worry about you, I really do."

"You needn't. I know what's best for me."

"If you say so. Good-bye for now, then."

"Good-bye, Barbara."

I put the phone down on the roller cart next to the rocker. I had been sitting here for a long time now, most of yesterday, all of last night, all of this morning. Not once had I had gotten up. There was no need for food because I wasn't hungry, no need to go to the bathroom because I hadn't eaten or drunk anything in some time. Nor had I gotten dressed since my outing to Safeway. Sitting in my robe in the light, the dark, the light again. Thinking sporadically now and then, but with my mind mostly a blank slate. Waiting for enough strength to move.

Barbara's news about the invader had provided it. I stood with difficulty, shuffled slowly into the bedroom, into the bathroom. For the first time in weeks I looked at my image in the medicine-cabinet mirror. The horse face seemed whole, if drawn and doughy, but that was illusion; it was nothing more than a mask hiding the shadow within. A mask that might have been made of wax, for the more closely I looked, the more the features seemed indistinct, as if they were beginning to melt into an unrecognizable mass.

I opened the cabinet to hide the mask and reached inside for the vials of Xanax and Vicodin. My fingers were steady as I removed the caps. Both containers were nearly full. I filled the water glass from the tap, swallowed a few of each of the tablets. Not too many at once or I might vomit them up. I refilled the glass, carried it and the two vials into the bedroom, and sat on the bed for a little time to make sure my stomach wouldn't rebel. Then I swallowed several more Xanax, several more Vicodin.

I had thought, during the long night, of writing a note. But what would I say to Barbara or Arthur or anyone that would have any meaning? How could I explain that the emptiness, the sense of self being reduced to shadows and invisibility, meant I was already dead and had been in soul and spirit since the night of the invasion?

When I began to feel sleepy, I lay back with my eyes closed to wait for the final darkness.

JENNA KELLS

I CONSIDER MYSELF A tolerant person. I know television and newspaper reporters have jobs to do, and I try to be cordial and cooperative with them. But I draw the line when they persistently hound Griffin and then come around and hound me by quoting disparaging remarks that have been made about his competency.

One particularly obnoxious woman is employed by the Riverton cable TV station, an adversarial type whose primary objective seems to be stirring up controversy in order to further her image and her career. She and her camera crew showed up at the house this afternoon, after conducting an interview with Mayor Delahunt. The disparaging remarks were his, of course. He had not only questioned Griff's abilities, referring to him as "a disappointment to the beleaguered citizens of Santa Rita," but outrageously implied that Griff's "failures" were partially responsible for the latest assault on Ted Lowenstein's daughter and indicated that his tenure as chief of police would end unless the rapist was quickly identified and arrested.

The woman took ill-concealed glee in relating this to me, clearly hoping for an inflammatory reaction. I could have given her one, complete with appropriate four-letter words, but I managed to restrain myself. I defended Griff quietly and politely, saying he and his officers had done and were doing everything humanly possible, and implied that he was the victim of a political witch hunt and that Mayor Delahunt was full of shit. Smiling all the while, the same sort of phony smile Delahunt assumes when he's dealing with the media."

Once the reporter and her crew were gone, I allowed myself a small private rant. Damn that smarmy political hack! Damn all the media lackeys! None of them knew Griff the way I did. They had no idea how hard he worked, how much he cared, how much harrying he'd been subjected to, the toll this series of crimes was taking on him physically and emotionally. No idea!

The rant made me feel a little better. But the empty house was having a claustrophobic effect on me now. What I needed was to talk to someone who understood how I felt, who was experiencing the same frustrations and sense of helplessness. Sofia Ortiz. On impulse I went out to the car and drove across town to the Ortiz home.

She was in, fortunately, and welcoming as always. We were friendly without being friends, drawn together by our husbands' jobs, but she and Robert were private people, as Griff and I were, and so we hadn't quite been able to bridge the racial, social, and familial differences between us. There was simply not enough common ground. Except for what had brought me here today.

I only wanted to talk, but Sofia insisted on serving coffee and sweet rolls in the living room. I told her about the TV reporter's visit, and what the mayor had said about Griff. She wasn't aware that Delahunt had included her husband in his disparaging remarks, and I didn't enlighten her. It would have been unkind.

"Have the media bothered you today, too?" I asked.

"They were here, yes. But I did not speak with them."

"I wish I hadn't. There's so much cruelty in the world without those people adding to it."

"Yes," she said, and her eyes were sad. "So much cruelty."

"How do you deal with it, Sofia?"

"With prayer. Every morning and every evening I pray."

"Sometimes it seems God isn't listening."

"Oh, but He is. He has answered my most important prayer."

"May I ask what that is?"

"That each night He sends Roberto home safely to me and our children."

I smiled and nodded. It must be a great comfort, I thought, to have faith as strong as hers. I wished mine were half as steadfast.

ROBERT ORTIZ

THE ASSAILANT HAD GIGGLED throughout his assault on Angela Lowenstein. Her word—*giggled.*

None of the other four victims had mentioned the perp giggling or laughing; I rechecked the interrogation transcripts to make certain. During each of those assaults the perp had been said to spew threats and foul language, to breathe heavily and grunt, but that was all.

She had also stated that he spoke rapidly, running his words together, and "panted like a dog." The cause of both might have been intense sexual excitement, but there was another possibility, too, which would explain the giggling—that he had been high on something. Not alcohol, or she would have smelled it on him and reported it. A controlled substance, the kind that can increase both aggressive behavior and sexual fervor.

When Griff returned from his meeting at the mayor's office, I went in to get his opinion. He did not want to discuss the details of the meeting, but I could guess how it had gone from the tension in his body language, the angry clenching of his jaw. What I had to say did not improve his disposition, though he was not unreceptive.

"I noticed the disparities, too," he said. "You may be right that the perp was high on some kind of drug, but that doesn't have to mean it's not the same man."

"It could, though."

"Perps change their MOs sometimes, you know that, Robert. On purpose or for circumstantial reasons. There were differences in each of the four previous assaults."

"But none as significant as this."

"You're not thinking copycat? *Two* crazies attacking women?"

"One new psycho, the other one dead."

He knuckle-massaged his tired eyes. "You just won't let up on Martin Torrey."

"Not unless we have conclusive proof that he wasn't guilty."

"Or conclusive proof that he was. All right. Let's suppose last night's assailant is a copycat. We're still left with two perps to track down— Angela Lowenstein's rapist and Torrey's murderer."

"He could be someone she knows," I said. "Her missing apartment key could have been stolen rather than lost. The fact that it disappeared two weeks ago is suspiciously coincidental."

"Granted. But coincidences do happen. And according to her statement, she never lets her purse out of her sight."

"*Never* is a word people sometimes use loosely, when what they really mean is hardly ever."

"No argument there."

"Another thing," I said. "When you asked her if the perp's voice was familiar to her, she did not rule out the possibility that it was."

"She didn't support it, either."

"Still, this could be something more than a copycat crime."

"How do you mean?"

"Personally motivated. All the serial trappings just a smoke screen."

Griff frowned. "Somebody with a grudge against Angela?"

"Yes. It seems certain she was targeted ahead of time."

"So was at least one of the other victims. Ione Spivey. Home invasion there, too. Targeted doesn't have to mean Angela knows him, or that he had a personal motive for assaulting her."

"No," I admitted, "it doesn't."

"Look, Robert, I don't want this to be the work of the serial any more than you do. I hope to God it isn't. But the public is going to think it is.

People were afraid enough before, but this assault is liable to start a panic. We've had one possible vigilante killing already. Christ knows what might happen if more lynch-law types start roaming the streets with guns."

He was right, of course. The tasks we faced and their potential consequences were the same no matter who had assaulted Angela Lowenstein or what his motive had been.

COURTNEY REEVES

I LIKE WORKING AT the Riverfront Brew Pub. Or I did until I was raped and my whole life started falling apart.

It's on the turning basin downtown, where boats come up the channel from the river and sometimes tie up for a night or two along the floats there—sailboats and small yachts and other kinds that are nice to look at. The patio's small, with about a dozen regular tables and picnic-type benches, and there are a few more tables in the inside section, so it's pretty easy to waitress there. It's where I met Jason. He'd been tending bar at Riverfront for about a year when they hired me. I liked him right away and played up to him until he asked me out, and I went to bed with him that same night. That was when I knew I loved him. And I thought he loved me, too, when he asked me to move in with him.

Now . . .

Now I was pretty sure I wouldn't be working at the Riverfront much longer. Or living with Jason much longer, either. I can put up with a lot, but not his lying to me and selling meth again and cheating on me even if he had some cause. Once we broke up, as we probably would, I wouldn't be able to stand seeing him almost every day. He wouldn't quit his job, so I'd have to quit mine. I'd have to be the one to move out and find some other place to live, too.

I almost didn't come to work today and I wish I hadn't. It was hard being here with him, knowing what I knew and feeling the way I did, and what made it even worse was the new rape last night everybody was talking about. Angela Lowenstein, the newspaper owner's daughter. Everybody was real upset about it. Customers were giving me looks and whispering again like they had after it happened to me, some feeling sorry for me with their eyes, a few acting like I had a contagious disease or something.

God, it was awful. The new rape meant Jason had been wrong and the rapist wasn't Martin Torrey after all. He didn't like being wrong about anything, especially something like this. He kept snapping and glaring at everybody, me most of all. As if it was my fault the rapist was still out there hurting other women and nobody had any idea who he was.

The day dragged on and on. There was a midafternoon slowdown, same as usual, only a couple of tables occupied on the patio—my section. I was out there taking an order for a couple of Lagunitas IPAs when the red-haired guy came in past the reception desk.

I'd never seen him before, but I didn't like his looks. He was dressed all right, in a shirt and slacks, but he had a funny, kind of spacey look, there was sweat on his face, and he moved in a jerky way. I'm real sensitive to how people look when they're stoned, now more than ever, and this guy was high on something and starting to come down. I knew it right away.

He went straight to the bar inside. I followed after him to give Jason the IPA order. There weren't any customers inside and Jason was standing behind the bar, fiddling with one of the draft spigots. But when he saw the red-haired dude he jumped like he'd been goosed or something.

"What the hell're you doing here?" he said in a low growl.

"Have to talk to you, nobody else around who can fix me up—"

"Not here, not now. Christ!"

The guy twitched up close to the bar, almost knocking over one of the stools. "Listen, I'm sorry about the other night, I shouldn't've gone off on you like that, but I—"

"I said not now!"

Jason saw me in the areaway and made a shooing motion with his hand, but I stayed where I was. My not obeying pissed him off even more. His teeth showed like a dog snarling.

"I'm all messed up," the guy said. "I need—"

"Shut up!"

Jason stomped down to the end of the bar, motioning for the guy to follow him, and then they both leaned over with their heads close and said some things back and forth in low voices. I couldn't make out most of it, but I did hear one thing—Pooch's name. Then Jason straightened up and I heard him say, "Now get your ass out of here. And don't come back!"

The red-haired guy came jerking and twitching my way. I moved quick then, off to one side, but he didn't even look at me as he went out. Jason stomped back to the row of spigots, and when I stepped up to the bar, he said, "What the hell's the matter with you? You had no business standing there with your ears flapping."

"Who is he, Jason? What did he want?"

He didn't answer. Just glared at me. The look in his eyes . . . God, it was almost as if he hated me.

The rest of our shift he didn't say a word to me. Sometimes I drive my car to work, but I hadn't today so I had to ride back to the apartment with him. Well, I didn't have to, I could've gotten a ride with somebody else, but I did because I had to find out some things so I could make up my mind what to do.

On the way out of the parking lot, I said, "Jason, I want to know who that red-haired guy was."

"None of your business."

"Roy, the one you had the fight with. Right?"

"Don't you understand plain English? None of your business."

"He was stoned," I said. "High on meth. I know the signs."

"You don't know shit."

"He wanted you to sell him some more, didn't he? That's why he came in all messed up."

"You're crazy. I don't sell crank or anything else."

"You sent him to Pooch."

"The hell I did."

"I think you did. I think you're using again and dealing again."

He didn't deny it a second time. He didn't say anything.

I took a deep breath. "I think you're cheating on me, too. Seeing another girl, screwing some other girl."

"Bullshit." But he gave me a quick sideways look before he said it. And the truth was right there on his face.

"I smelled her on you," I said. "All over you. Dealing meth is bad enough, but being unfaithful is worse. Unforgivable the way things are with me right now. Why couldn't you wait?"

"Wait," he said. "Wait for you to finally get over being raped? Wait for something that might never happen?"

That hurt, really hurt. "You don't care about me anymore, do you?"

No answer.

"No, you don't. All you care about is yourself. Getting high, getting money, getting laid."

"Shut up, Courtney. I don't need this kind of crap from you."

"I don't need your crap, either."

"You don't like me the way I am, maybe it's time we called it quits."

"Maybe it is."

"Well, I'm not gonna be the one to move out."

"No, I will."

"Where the hell would you go? Back to live with that drunken old lady of yours?"

"She may be a drunk, but at least she gives a shit about me and my feelings."

Neither of us had anything more to say until he pulled up in front of the apartment building. "All right, get out," he said then. "I've got things to do."

"Sell meth to Roy, screw your new girlfriend."

"Maybe. Yeah, maybe."

"And maybe I won't be here when you get back."

"So go if you want to. Just make sure you take that stupid goddamn dog with you."

He drove off with tires squealing. I went into the apartment and hugged Ladybug and fed her and then took her for a quick walk, and after I got back I started packing up my things. I didn't have all that much so it didn't take me long. I was still so hurt, so mad. But I was all through crying, all through loving Jason. All through being a victim.

There wasn't anything I could do about the rapist and what he'd done to me, but I could do something about Jason.

I could get even.

SHERRY WILDER

So the bastard isn't dead after all. He attacked another woman last night, victim number five. Whoever killed Martin Torrey shot the wrong man.

I heard about it from Sam Norden. I decided it was about time I started working out again, and I went in to Norden's Fitness this morning and he told me as soon as I walked in. He was pretty upset. So were his customers, especially the women. One of them, a chubby matron I'd never seen before, said the dirty rapist ought to be castrated on the spot when they caught him and then allowed to bleed to death, and that she'd volunteer to do the slicing and dicing. I agreed with her suggestion, but not with her method. Martin Torrey's killer had the right idea. The Pink Lady and I would gladly, joyously shoot off his cock and balls, blow them into tiny bloody pieces. But of course we'd never be given the opportunity. Not with him, anyway.

The news depressed me, and a strenuous workout on the cross-trainers and ellipticals didn't help me feel any better. It was only eleven o'clock when I left Norden's. I thought about driving down to Riverton for some target practice at Bull's-Eye, but the place was so popular you had to make reservations to use the range. Besides, Tina would be busy working with other shooters—she was the most popular instructor they had. It wouldn't be any fun practicing with one of the other instructors.

I checked my voice mail. Three messages, two from women friends wanting to talk about the attack last night, and one from Neal. I didn't listen to Neal's. He'd be calling about the rape, too, and knowing him, he'd suggest we get together for lunch so we could talk about it . . . *he* could talk about it. No way. I didn't want to hear his voice, much less spend even five minutes with him in the middle of the day.

It was too early for lunch but not too early for Johnnie Walker. I drove over to the Santa Rita Inn and drank two doubles at the bar, taking my time with the second. But Johnnie didn't bring me out of the doldrums, either. Around noon people started coming into the lounge, men in suits, men with roving eyes, and what they were thinking when they looked at me was as plain as if they were saying the words out loud. I wanted another drink, but not here, not with them and their dirty minds and leering mouths. It would be the same any other place I went, and I wasn't hungry and I didn't feel like company, so I just went on home.

The landline was ringing when I got there. I let the answering machine pick up because it was sure to be Neal again. Right, it was. Wondering why I hadn't called back and if I was all right. He sounded half-worried and half-pissed-off. Well, let him wonder. I erased him from the machine as soon as his message ended, along with two others that I didn't listen to.

The weather was fairly warm, so I sat out on the side terrace with Johnnie, and after a while I fell asleep. It was nearly three when I woke up. I was still depressed, a pounding headache and a sour stomach making it worse. I went inside and showered and put on a caftan. My Baggallini was on the bureau; I took the Pink Lady out and sat on the bed holding her for a few minutes. She made me feel a little better.

I made myself eat a piece of toast with cream cheese to stop the acidic grumbling in my stomach. You have to eat sometime, as my father used to say. He'd had a full complement of clichés like that, Pop had. In a way he'd even died of one—a sudden heart attack while he was on the golf course, getting ready to miss another short putt. I still missed him, but not as much as I had right after he died.

Time for another communion with Johnnie. Maybe he would help cure the headache, if not the damn depression. But he didn't. I was on my third round, sitting on the family room couch with my feet up, my temples still beating like a tom-tom, when Neal came home.

"There you are," he said when he saw me. "Where have you been all day?"

"Out. And now back in."

"That's no answer."

"It's the only one you're going to get."

He gave me one of his exasperated pinch-mouthed looks. "I called your cell and the house several times. Why didn't you answer or call back?"

"No reason to. I already knew what happened last night."

"Who told you?"

"Sam Norden. If it matters."

"It does if you were at the gym today."

"Why?"

"You always enjoyed working out, teaching, before—"

"Go ahead and say it. Before I was buggered and sliced up like a piece of raw meat."

"Sherry, please . . ."

"Sherry please what? That's what happened, isn't it?"

"You don't have to keep dwelling on it."

"No? How am I supposed to stop dwelling on it? He's still out there buggering and slicing up other women, isn't he?"

"Yes, dammit. I was so sure Martin Torrey was the one and the whole nightmare was over and we could start living a normal life again—"

"*We* could?"

"All right, you could."

"The kind of so-called normal life you're talking about is dead and gone, beyond resurrection."

"It doesn't have to be. You can still pick up the pieces."

"Pick up the pieces. You're just like my father, you know that? Full of stupid clichés."

"I'm only trying to be supportive." The exasperated pinch-mouthed look again. "Why do you keep fighting me, turning everything I say around, making every conversation confrontational?"

I didn't say anything. My head was pounding, pounding.

"Sherry, if you'd only—"

"Oh, for God's sake, go away and leave me alone!"

I shut my eyes so I wouldn't have to look at him. I heard him go over to the wet bar, ice and glass clinking as he made himself a drink. *If he sits down next to me, I'll scream.* But he didn't. He did what I'd told him and went away, out of the family room into some other part of the house.

When I was sure he was gone, I got up and refilled my glass. I had to pee, so I carried Johnnie with me into the guest bathroom. I was back in the family room when I heard the sudden thumping noise, not loud but loud enough to carry from one of the other rooms. I didn't think anything of it until I heard Neal exclaim, "Jesus Christ!" As if he'd hurt himself or something.

But that wasn't it. Oh, no, the reason he'd yelled was much worse than that.

He came storming into the family room, his face flushed and his eyes snapping. "What the hell are you doing with this?"

He had the Pink Lady in the palm of his hand.

The way he was holding her, as if she were something obscene like a dead rat, made me so furious my head felt as if it were about to explode. "Snooping in my bag, you son of a bitch!"

"I wasn't snooping, I accidentally knocked it off the dresser and this thing fell out. Where did you get it? When?"

"I bought her, I've had her for weeks."

"Her?"

"She's a Pink Lady."

"Pink Lady. Christ Almighty! A pink gun! Have you lost your mind? You know how I feel about guns."

"I don't give a shit how you feel about guns. All that matters is how I feel about them now."

"You never fired one in your life—"

"Oh, yes, I have. Hundreds of times the past few weeks." I put my glass down on the table and started toward him. "Give her to me."

"No. I won't let you have—"

He didn't expect me to lunge at him, but that's exactly what I did. I clawed his arm with my left hand and snatched the Pink Lady with my right and then started to back away with her. But the stupid idiot reached out and caught at my wrist and tried to take her back.

And she went off.

All by herself, it seemed. Just went off.

The crack of the shot and the smack of the bullet's hitting something and Neal's yell were all mixed up together. At first I thought he was shot, but there wasn't any blood on him and he didn't clutch at himself or fall down. He just stood there with his face the color of smoke and ashes and his eyes bulging like a character's in a horror film.

"My God," he said. "My God, the bullet almost took my ear off."

Yes, it had. There was a hole in the wall behind and a little to one side of his head.

"Don't ever touch her again," I said. "Or next time she might not go off by accident."

He kept on staring at me in that bug-eyed way. "I don't know you anymore. I don't want to know you anymore."

"You never knew me. And I don't want to know you anymore, either."

I stepped around him and took the Pink Lady into the bedroom and put her back in the Baggallini where she belonged.

HAROLD INGERSOLL

I ALMOST MISSED SEEING the bundle. And almost didn't stop to look at it when I did spot it.

It was underneath one of the benches on the walkway above the boat slips, more or less in plain sight if you were looking down in that direction. It was some kind of cloth bundle, a grubby-white color, pushed up against one of the bench's wrought-iron supports. A garbage can stood on the other side, a few feet away, and my first thought was that somebody had tossed the bundle at the can and missed and just left it where it lay.

Well, I'm not usually nosy. Particularly when I'm on my way home from a relaxing day cruise on *River Nymph* and some pretty good fishing down in the marshes. It's not often I can take a day off during the week—the real estate business keeps you hopping—but I had a clear schedule today. Some men's passion is golf, boating is mine. And *River Nymph* is my pride and joy—a sleek Ebbtide Cuddy Bow Rider, 430 horses, the sweetest little craft in the entire North Park Marina if I do say so myself.

So I started to walk on by the bench, but something about that bundle stuck with me and finally made me turn back. I sat on the edge of the bench and reached under to pull it out. It was about a foot long; the cloth, a thin towel of some kind, wrapped around whatever was inside. The towel had an oily feel. It was damp, too, as if it had been lying there in the grass overnight or maybe even longer. That could be, because not a lot of boat owners come down to the marina during the week, and those who do aren't as observant as I am.

There was something sharp inside the bundle; when I picked it up and started to unwind it, it nicked my finger right through the cloth. That almost made me toss it over into the garbage can unopened. But curiosity got the best of me. I went ahead and finished unwrapping it, being much more careful while I was doing it.

When I saw what was in there, my jaw unhinged and I jumped up so fast I nearly dropped it all on the ground.

Jesus, Mary, and Joseph!

Black-and-white ski mask. Pair of black leather gloves. And a knife, a hunting knife with an eight-inch blade stained at the tip . . . reddish-brown stains . . . bloodstains.

Naturally the first thing I thought of was the rapes. What else could these things be but what the sicko had used? Why he'd abandoned them here was puzzling, but I didn't stop to think about it; it wasn't my business, it was police business. I wrapped up the bundle again, being extra-careful, and half ran to where I'd parked my car.

SUSAN SINCLAIR

I RETURNED TO THE hospital for another visit with Angela Lowenstein late that afternoon. I wanted to see how she was doing, and I had a few more questions to ask her.

She seemed glad to see me. As though I were a friend and not just another police officer who also happened to be a victims' advocate. That was good, the way it should be. She'd bonded with me because I am a woman, because I understood what she was going through from a personal as well as a professional perspective—I'd been date-raped when I was nineteen, though I hadn't told her that—and the compassion I communicated to her was genuine. I'm not always able to establish that kind of bond with a female crime victim, particularly in cases of violent assault and domestic abuse. I'd succeeded with only two of the other victims in the serial rapes, Ione Spivey and Courtney Reeves; the others had withdrawn into themselves, kept the anger and bitterness and shame walled up instead of letting me, among other professionals, try to help ease it.

Victims' advocate is the most difficult part of my job. Yet it can also be the most rewarding. When Dad accepted that I was serious about following him and Granddad into police work, one of the things he drummed into my head was that faithfully and honestly serving and protecting the public wasn't enough. That what made you a good cop was the desire and the effort to make a difference, even if it was only a small one, in the lives of the people you dealt with. That credo was the reason I'd volunteered for the VA position. I've lived by it my whole career.

Angela looked better than she had earlier, some color in her cheeks, not as much pain clouding her eyes. The sadness, the emotional turmoil, were still palpable, of course. They would fade in time, but unlike her physical injuries, the psychic wounds would never fully heal; the scar tissue that formed would be thin, breakable under the wrong kind of pressure, like scabs over long-festering sores. Knowing this, confronting it, not only deepened my empathy but made me angry, too. Not just at the perp, not just at all men who abused women, but at men in general. Rape, especially this string of vicious serial rapes, has that effect on me. Thank God I was married to a kind, gentle man like George. Otherwise my perspective might have become permanently warped.

I smiled at Angela. The expression and tone of voice I'd learned to cultivate at times like this were neither solemn nor cheerful, but somewhere in between. Upbeat, but not happy-face.

"How are you feeling?" The standard opener.

"Better. The doctor says I can go home tomorrow."

"Not back to your apartment?"

"No. My dad's house. He wants me to stay with him for a while."

"Good. That's a wise decision." I sat on one of the visitors' chairs. "I've been thinking about what you told us this morning and there's something I'm wondering about. Do you mind a few more questions?"

"No. Not if it'll help."

"It concerns your apartment key, the one attached to the dream catcher. You said you kept it in your purse. Is that always the case? Never anywhere else, such as a coat or jacket pocket?"

"No. Only in my purse."

"Inside, or in a zipper compartment?"

"Zipper compartment, usually. But I must have just dropped it inside the day I lost it."

"Your purse is always with you, everywhere you go?"

"Yes. Restaurants, clubs, school . . . everywhere."

"What about at the *Clarion*? Ever leave it when you were away from your desk?"

"No. Well . . . I might have, once in a while, when Daddy called me into his office or I had a sudden need to use the bathroom."

"Where would you have left it those times? On top of the desk, in a drawer?"

"I'm not sure. In the bottom drawer, probably, that's where I usually keep it when I'm working."

"What's the location of your desk? Do you have a private office?"

"Not really. Just a little alcove at the back of the newsroom, near Daddy's office."

"Things must get pretty hectic there sometimes."

"Sometimes."

"Hectic enough to keep you away from your desk for several minutes?"

"Now and then, yes."

"The day the apartment key went missing?"

"I don't remember . . . maybe . . ."

"So someone could have sat down there briefly while you were away without anybody noticing. Opened your purse and taken the key."

She nodded, then blinked and winced as she shifted position. "You don't think . . . One of *Clarion* staff? A man I work with?"

"You told us the assailant's voice might have been familiar. And it would explain how he managed to gain access to your apartment without breaking in."

"Yes, but . . . my God."

"Did any of the men ever make advances to you?"

"Advances? No."

"Ask you for a date, act more than just naturally friendly?"

"No." Again she paused. "Well, there is one guy, he's only been at the paper a few months. He never came on to me or anything, but a couple of times I caught him looking at me. A lot of guys look at me, I never thought anything of it . . ."

"What about him?"

"I overheard him say something once . . . not to me, about me."

"What was it?"

"That I was stuck-up—" A look of horror altered her expression, the kind brought on by a sudden memory flash. "*He* said that just before he raped me. He called me a 'stuck-up bitch.'"

I was already on my feet. "What's his name, the guy in the office?"

"Smith. Royce Smith."

PART FOUR

SATURDAY, APRIL 23–
SUNDAY, APRIL 24

GRIFFIN KELLS

WE COULDN'T QUESTION ROYCE Smith because we couldn't find him.

As soon as Sergeant Sinclair phoned in her report last night, Robert and Al Bennett had gone to Smith's apartment on Alvarado Street. He wasn't there, and his neighbors had no idea where he might be. The building was staked out, but Smith didn't return during the night or this morning. I contacted Tyler James at the *Clarion*; Smith wasn't there, either. Hadn't been in or phoned in, James said, for the past two days. No one on the staff had been close to him. Kept mostly to himself—a quiet loner. James was full of questions, but I was not about to divulge why we were interested in Smith because I didn't want it to get back to Ted Lowenstein. There was no point in raising both his hopes and his ire at this preliminary stage.

I asked James for some background information on Smith, which he supplied. Born in Chico, had a journalism degree from Chico State, but aside from sports reporting for the college paper, hardly any practical experience until Lowenstein hired him a few months ago. His father and mother still lived in Chico. We ran his name through NICS and the California justice system. One hit, an arrest in Butte County for mari-juana possession. A call to his parents' home bought us nothing; his mother claimed he hadn't been in touch with the family in over a year, and she didn't seem particularly unhappy about it. She didn't know the names of any of his friends there or in Santa Rita. If he had any friends, she said. The DMV provided the license number of Smith's vehicle, a beige 2008 Hyundai Elantra SE, and we put out a BOLO alert on it and on him. We didn't have enough on him to make it an APB.

If he was the man who had criminally assaulted Angela Lowenstein, was he also the rapist in the other four cases? Robert didn't think so—as focused as ever on Martin Torrey—but I still held out a small hope that all five assaults were the work of the same man. If that was the case and we could prove it, it would relieve the heaviest of the pressure weighing us down. Then we could devote all our efforts to the Torrey homicide.

Now we had another complication to deal with—the bundle the real estate agent, Harold Ingersoll, had found at North Park Marina and brought in last night. Rapist's tools, undoubtedly, but whose? Smith's, if he was guilty of at least the Lowenstein assault? That seemed the most likely explanation for their having been abandoned—a one-and-done perp getting rid of the evidence. But why leave the bundle in plain sight in such a public spot? Why not bury it somewhere or weight it down and pitch it into the river? It was as though the bundle was meant to be found.

Robert put forth another theory: that the tools belonged to the serial, to Martin Torrey; that one of his relatives had found them and dumped them to prevent the truth from coming out. A stretch, as far as I was concerned. If Torrey was the serial, he'd have had the tools secreted somewhere nobody would be likely to stumble across them. Robert had an answer for that, too. The missing key with the red dot. Torrey's wife could have known or suspected he was guilty, removed the key from his ring not long before he was killed because she knew what it opened, and retrieved the bundle. Again, a stretch. And what it didn't explain was the careless abandonment at the marina. You don't try to protect a loved one by leaving incriminating evidence in a place where it's likely to be found.

We'd know more when the contents of the bundle were forensically examined. Even if the knife had been washed with soap or soaked in solvent, microscopic blood traces would be on the blade. In which case a DNA match would determine whether it had been used on one or more of the victims. But tests of that sort were beyond Joe Bloom's and our lab equipment's capabilities; it was the weekend again and Ed Braverman and his crew wouldn't be able to make the blood-sample tests until next week, and it takes time, often a long time, to get DNA results.

What Joe could do here was run tests on the ski mask and gloves and the cloth towel. There was some sort of oily residue on the towel that he thought he might be able to identify. Part of his state P.O.S.T. technician's certification included knowledge of forensic chemistry.

I spent what was left of the morning avoiding unnecessary phone calls and media requests and attending to other departmental matters. At twelve thirty I sent out for a sandwich I didn't want. I was nibbling on it, washing it down with coffee loaded with milk and sugar to cut down on the caffeine, when more bad news came in.

One of the rape victims, the unmarried schoolteacher, Eileen Jordan, had been found deceased in her cottage. Overdose of prescription medications. Suicide.

A friend, Barbara Jacobs, had tried phoning her this morning because Miss Jordan had seemed depressed when they last talked and she was worried about her. When she got no answer, she drove to the cottage to check and found the front door unlocked, the woman lying dead on her bed. Deceased since sometime yesterday, apparently, according to the coroner's estimate. Mostly empty pill bottles on a nightstand in the bedroom. No note found as yet.

The food soured in my stomach. I threw the rest of the sandwich into the wastebasket.

Poor battered, shattered Eileen Jordan. Fifty years old. Lived alone, suffered alone, died alone.

A self-administered drug overdose would go down as the official cause of death. But rape—brutal, inhuman rape—was the real cause.

If it were up to me, her exit from this world would go into the record as a homicide.

SHERRY WILDER

NEAL SPENT THE NIGHT in the guest room or on the couch in the living room, I don't know or care which, and he came into the bedroom and woke me up at eight thirty. He was dressed like it was a weekday. He even had his briefcase in one hand.

"I'm going to see Mel Vincent this morning," he said. His lawyer and golf buddy. "I'm sure it won't come as any surprise to you that I'm filing for divorce."

"Fast worker. Beat me to it."

"I can't live with you anymore, Sherry."

"Likewise. I can't say it was fun while it lasted because it wasn't."

"You're not the same person you were before the assault. I can't give you the kind of help you need, but if you don't find somebody who can—"

"Don't preach at me, goddamn you." My head ached from too much Johnnie, and now that Neal had woken me up and denied me the pleasure of filing for the divorce myself, I felt sullen and snappish. "I've got what I need. Or I will have once I'm rid of you."

"Too much scotch and now a gun. Recipe for disaster."

"Oh, shut up. Go on, get out of here."

But he didn't go yet. More talk. Talk, talk, talk. "There are some things we have to decide. About living arrangements, about the house—"

"I don't want your damn architect's wet-dream house, if that's what's worrying you. Not even for a little while. I'll move out just as soon as I can find a place. And you can move Gloria Ryder in."

"How many times do I have to tell you I'm not having an affair with Gloria Ryder. Or anybody else."

"I don't give a shit anymore, one way or the other. Can't you get that through *your* head?"

"All right, then. What do you want in the divorce?"

"What I'm entitled to in this good old community-property state— half of our liquid assets, my share of what the house is worth. And my car. You can have all the rest."

"Don't you want the wet bar?" Neal said nastily.

"Fuck the wet bar." *And fuck you, too.*

"I think I'd better stay in a motel until you move out. I'll be back to pack after I talk to Mel."

"I won't be here."

"That would be best." He turned, then stopped. He was looking at the Baggallini. He said in that same nasty way, "Pink Lady. Christ!"

"That's right. My Pink Lady."

"I hope the two of you will be happy together," he said, and went out and finally left me alone.

I stayed in bed for a while until my head stopped throbbing, then got up and showered and put on my black slacks and loose pullover. What I wanted to do more than anything else today was to drive to Riverton and take target practice at Bull's-Eye. I didn't know if Tina instructed on Saturdays, but I hoped she did. It would make my day if she was there.

I wondered what she'd say when I told her about the divorce. I was looking forward to finding out.

COURTNEY REEVES

W HEN I GOT TO the police station, I almost didn't go inside.
I sat in the parking lot and looked at it and I couldn't seem to
make myself open the car door. My palms were all sweaty. I'd stayed up
most of the night at Ma's house thinking, and I was pretty sure I'd made
the right decisions. I had to stick by them. If I didn't . . . well, then I'd go
on being a victim.

I'd already started by calling my aunt Dorothy in Salem, Oregon. I
hadn't seen her since high school graduation, but we'd always gotten
along pretty well, better than I got along with Ma. She didn't know that
I'd been raped; I thought Ma had told her, but she hadn't, which figured.
Aunt Dorothy was horrified. And when I told her about my troubles with
Jason, right away she said yes, I could come stay with her for a while and
she'd help me find a job up there.

There wasn't anything for me in Santa Rita anymore, just ugly memories that blacked out all the good ones. If I was ever going to get over
being raped, it would have to be in some place far away from here where
I could have a whole new life. Ma wouldn't care if I moved away. All she
cared about was having a good time and hooking up with guys who
bought her drinks. As it was, I hardly saw her. She probably wouldn't miss
me at all.

So that part of it was settled. Then I'd called the Riverfront and told
them I wouldn't be in today, that I was going to be moving to Oregon

soon, and I'd be in to get my last paycheck before I left. I was going to need that money. I didn't have much, only a few dollars left over from my last check and a few more that I'd kept at the apartment for food and stuff. Then I'd gotten ready and come down here to the police station.

I'd never been inside it before. After I was raped, the police came to see me at the hospital or the apartment. And I'd never been arrested or gone there to visit anyone who had, including Ma the two times she'd been picked up for being drunk in public. It was kind of a scary place. I mean, Jason hates cops, even the ones like Sergeant Sinclair who helped me, and so I've been leery of them, too. But I liked Sergeant Sinclair, she was real easy to talk to. I just hoped she was here today. I should've called to find out. And then if she was, maybe I could have said what I had to say to her on the phone. Except I knew it would be better saying it in person, face-to-face, so here I was.

I'd brought Ladybug along and she looked up at me, then put her paw on my leg as if she were urging me to go ahead, get out of the car, go inside. What a sweetie she was, my only true friend now except for Aunt Dorothy. I patted her, kissed her, got myself together, and went into the station.

It wasn't as noisy inside as I expected it would be. There wasn't anybody there except a cop in uniform behind the counter. He was friendly enough, but he told me what I didn't want to hear. Sergeant Sinclair wasn't on duty today. Was there anybody else who could help me?

Well, I almost said no. Almost turned around and walked out. But I needed to talk to somebody before I could change my mind, so Lieutenant Ortiz's name popped out of my mouth. He's kind of imposing, I guess that's the word, but he'd always been nice enough to me, if not to Jason. I guessed I could talk to him all right. And he *was* on duty.

The uniformed cop asked me the nature of my business, I told him it had to do with a serious crime that the lieutenant should know about. He passed that on, and about two minutes later I was sitting in Lieutenant Ortiz's office. My hands were still sweating. Otherwise, I was okay. And just as determined to go through with this as I had been last night and this morning. Don't get mad, get even. That's what they say, and they're right.

"The serious crime you have to report, Ms. Reeves, does it have anything to do with the criminal assaults?"

"No. It . . . well, it has to do with Jason. My ex-boyfriend."

"Ex?"

"We broke up last night. On account of what he's started doing again."

"And that would be?"

"You won't tell him I'm the one who told on him? Or make me testify against him in court or anything like that?"

"Do you have specific knowledge of a crime he's committed?"

"I'm not sure what you mean *specific*."

"Did you witness the commission of a crime? Have prior knowledge of it?"

"No."

"Then you needn't worry. Your name will not be revealed."

"That's a relief. See, I'll be leaving Santa Rita pretty soon, moving up to Oregon to live with my aunt, starting a new life—"

"What is it you have to tell me?"

I took a deep breath. "Jason is selling meth again," I said. "At least, I'm pretty sure he's selling it. I *know* he's been using it."

"He's brought drugs into your home?"

"Maybe he has, I'm not sure about that because I haven't seen any. But he stayed out late the past few nights and come home high twice . . . high on speed. I know where he's getting it."

"And where is that?"

"From Pooch," I said.

"Pooch. Who is he?"

"His real name is Pooch-insky, something like that. Lennie Pooch-insky. That's why he's called Pooch. He kind of looks like one, too, a fat, ugly mongrel dog."

Lieutenant Ortiz wrote something down, Pooch's name, probably. He looked real big sitting behind his desk, his face all dark and stern. And I felt small, like the time I got sent to the principal's office for spitting on another girl when I was in sixth grade. He'd been dark and stern, too, the principal, only he hadn't been Mexican.

"Where does this Pooch live?"

"On a run-down farm across the river," I said. "Jason told me he inherited it from some relative."

"A farm across the river. Where, exactly?"

"Dobler Road. I was there for a party once, that's how I know. Not a drug party," I lied quickly. The lieutenant just looked at me and I could feel my face getting hot. "Well, not meth anyway. I mean . . ."

"Does Pooch have a lab at his farm?"

"Lab? Oh, you mean, does he cook meth there. I think so, yes."

"But you're not sure."

"Pretty sure. That's where Jason goes to party with Pooch and other guys. Girls, too . . . He's been, you know, having sex with some other girl, that's another reason I broke up with him . . ."

"Can you tell me their names?"

"The girls? No. I don't want to know who they are, I don't care."

"The men?"

"No. Well, there's this guy Jason got into a fight with the other night when they were both cranked up. Probably over at Pooch's farm. Jason said he was one of these guys who got aggressive when he was stoned. I was surprised when he showed up at the brew pub to see Jason."

"When was that?"

"Yesterday afternoon. Jason was really pissed . . . mad, but not because of the fight. The guy was strung out, I think he wanted to buy some speed. He wasn't there very long. I think Jason sent him to Pooch."

"Do you know this man's name?"

"Just his first name. Roy."

"What did he look like?"

"Not very big, sort of average. He had red hair."

Now Lieutenant Ortiz looked even bigger, more imposing, his jaw jutting out like a hunk of rock. "Are you sure his name was Roy?"

"Well, it wasn't Ray or anything like that—"

"Could it have been Royce? R-o-y-c-e."

"I guess it could've been. Jason kind of mumbles sometimes . . ."

He stood up, doing it kind of fast like he was in a hurry all of a sudden.

He thanked me and said I'd done the right thing, coming in and talking to him. Then he said I'd have to postpone my move to Oregon, at least for a short time, in case he needed to talk to me again. Well, that was all right, so long as he kept his promise not to tell Jason it was me that turned him in. Ma wouldn't care if I stayed with her a few more days. I wasn't afraid Jason would try to hurt me if he did find out, he wouldn't dare because it'd make things a lot worse for him, but I didn't want to see or talk to him ever again.

When you stop loving somebody, you stop forever and that's that. The person just doesn't exist for you anymore. And that goes double when you're hoping to start a brand-new life in a brand-new place.

GRIFFIN KELLS

"ROY IS ROYCE SMITH," Robert said. "The Reeves girl's description matches. The man who assaulted Angela Lowenstein likely was high on drugs, and Smith is evidently an aggressive speed freak. He knew her, he had access in the *Clarion* office to her purse and apartment key. He's our man."

I nodded agreement. "About time we had something go our way. Now we've got to find him. The Reeves girl told you Palumbo sent him to see this Pooch yesterday?"

"That was the impression she got."

"Smith might still be there. What's Pooch's real name?"

"Puchinsky. Leonard Puchinsky. Property records on the Dobler Road parcel list him as the owner."

"Dobler Road. That's out in the county."

"Most of it. Not the address for the farm. It's located in the section the city annexed several years ago, close to the county line."

"Still our jurisdiction, then." A relief, that. If the farm had been on county land, I would have had to call in Sheriff Ritter, and he'd have insisted on assuming control. "The problem is, we don't have any concrete evidence that Puchinsky is running a meth lab on the property."

"No, but there's not much doubt. I ran a record check on him after the property check. One arrest and conviction in San Benito County five

years ago, before he inherited the farm and moved here, for manufac-
turing meth in a rented house."

"That's still not enough to convince a judge to give us a search warrant
for the farm."

"I can go out there, reconnoiter the place."

"Let's see what Palumbo can tell us first. He might know where Smith
is, if not at the farm."

"He bartends at the Riverfront Brew Pub on Saturdays. I'll call
Al Bennett—"

"No," I said, "let Al have his day off. I'll go with you. I'm tired of
sitting on my hands, waiting for something to happen."

Instead of Robert's cruiser or mine, we took one of the unmarked cars
the department used for surveillance. No point in giving advance warning
to Palumbo, or anyone at the Puchinsky farm if we ended up going there.
Robert did the driving.

Locating Palumbo proved no easier than locating Royce Smith. He
wasn't at the brew pub; he'd called in sick. He wasn't at his apartment
behind the football stadium, either.

"Check out the farm now?" Robert asked.

"Right. If we can get onto the property legally and Puchinsky's there,
we'll ask about Smith and see what kind of response we get."

"It might be a good idea to have some backup on standby, just in case."

"That it might."

I radioed in two orders—a BOLO alert on Jason Palumbo and his
blue Ford Mustang, the license number of which Robert had gotten from
the DMV earlier; and that the nearest patrol car to 1900 Dobler Road
establish a holding position in the immediate vicinity, but out of sight of
the farm buildings. Then we drove on through town and across the bridge
into the semirural, annexed section of town.

Nineteen hundred Dobler Road looked to be a couple of acres of
property butted right up against the county line. Beyond it lay hay and
alfalfa fields and, farther on, the vineyards that had sprouted on the little
hills and valleys near the river. Leonard Puchinsky's nearest neighbor
in that direction was a farm half a mile distant. The closest neighbor in

the section we'd just passed through was an auto dismantler's, with a couple hundred yards of rocky grassland between its junkyard fence and a straggly line of eucalyptus trees bordering the farm's access road.

The place was made-to-order for the kind of illegal business Puchinsky was evidently running. No one nearby to notice an unusual number of people coming and going at odd hours, and virtually no patrols by either SRPD officers or sheriff's deputies because of the proximity to the county line.

Robert said, "Ideal location for a meth lab."

"I was just thinking the same thing."

The rickety gate at the entrance stood wide-open—a bold welcome sign for Puchinsky's customers that suited us just as well. Robert turned in and we jounced along the unpaved, weed-sprinkled drive. The farm buildings lay bunched at an angle to the right—a one-story house, a small barn, a pump house. A few stunted apple trees grew beyond the barn; otherwise no vegetation was visible aside from grass and weeds. Even from a distance you could see that the farmhouse needed paint, a new front porch, a new roof. The barn was in better shape, no gapped or missing boards, its closed doors reinforced with lumber that hadn't had time to weather the same smoke gray as the rest of it. That was where the lab would be.

Puchinsky had plenty of company this afternoon. Four vehicles were parked off to one side of the house. When we got close enough for a clear look at them, I leaned forward with the muscles in my neck and back pulling tight.

One of the vehicles was a blue Mustang.

The other was a beige Hyundai Elantra SE.

ROBERT ORTIZ

I RECOGNIZED THE SUSPECTS' vehicles at the same time Griff did. "How do you want to proceed?" I asked him.

"Let's see what kind of reception we get and take it from there. Best approach is to try to pry Smith out of the house voluntarily. Palumbo can wait."

"We can't afford to push too hard without a warrant."

"No. Or to say anything about meth, cooking or selling."

There was no telling how many weapons might be on the premises, or if the people inside the house were high on drugs. The actions of manufacturers and users of methamphetamines are unpredictable. We already had ample hearsay evidence of Royce Smith's aggressive behavior while on heavy doses of speed.

I slowed to a crawl as we entered the farmyard, turned toward where the other vehicles were parked, and stopped there. We stepped out into a cool wind blowing in from across the river. We both had our coats open, the tails covering our holstered Glock service weapons and our hands in plain sight. If our arrival had alerted anyone inside the house or barn, they had not yet appeared.

"Somebody's bound to be watching us," Griff said. "They already know who we are—the way we're dressed would've told them that."

I said, "If we go to the door, we'll only get it slammed in our faces. If it's opened at all."

"Yeah. They can stay in there no matter what we do. But they've got to be wondering why we're here, what we want. If I were Puchinsky, I'd be itching to find out."

We crossed the dusty yard to the foot of the porch steps. The front windows wore shades, but I thought I saw movement at the edge of one. A lull in the wind brought the faint mutter of voices from inside, but they cut off abruptly. The only sounds then were the wind's whispering and the ratchety turning of the blades in a rusted windmill behind the pump house. In my ears, its rhythm was like the beating of a diseased heart.

Nothing happened for half a minute or so. The house door opened then and a man stepped out onto the porch. Late twenties, fat, his belly hanging and swaying when he moved. Long mud-colored hair tied in a ponytail. Sloppily dressed in Levi's and a stained sweatshirt. If he was worried, he did not show it. He leaned indolently against the support pole for the porch roof. His expression was guardedly neutral.

Griff said, "Leonard Puchinsky?"

"That's me."

"Police officers. I'm Chief Griffin Kells, this is Lieutenant Ortiz."

"Yeah, I know. I seen your pictures. So what brings you to my place?"

"Royce Smith."

". . . Who?"

"Royce Smith. The owner of that beige Hyundai over there."

"Oh, him. What you want him for?"

"Ask him to step out here."

"Why? He do something?"

"We need to talk to him."

"Yeah? What if he don't want to talk to you?"

"It would be in his best interest if he complies."

"You gonna arrest him? You got a warrant?"

"No. This is a routine field investigation."

"Whatever that is."

"Are you going to cooperate, Mr. Puchinsky?"

"This is private property, man. I don't have to do nothing you say unless you got a warrant."

"Then we'll go get one," Griff lied, bluffing. "And it won't be just for Royce Smith."

Puchinsky ceased leaning against the post, stood up straight. "You got no reason to hassle me—"

"We're not hassling you, we're asking you to cooperate. Is there some reason you don't want Smith to come out and talk to us?"

Puchinsky wiped a hand over his mouth, then swept it down across the bulge of his belly. His bluster was gone now. I could almost see the play of his thoughts behind dim eyes sunk in pouches of fat: Did we know about the meth lab? Were we after him, too?

"No," he said. "I don't hardly know him. Friend of a friend."

"Then go ask him to come out."

"All right. And then you take him outta here and leave me alone."

Without waiting for a response Puchinsky turned and reentered the house.

After a short silence, two male voices rose inside. One of them shouted, "No no no, no fucking way!" Then other voices rose into an alarmed babbling. Someone—Puchinsky, I thought—yelled, "Hey, what the hell you think you're doing—!" A loud crash then, followed by a cry of pain. Another shout: "Look out, look out, he's got a gun!" A woman began screaming.

Griff and I were already moving by then, back across the yard, hands on our weapons in response to that last ominous shout. Before we'd gone halfway, the sounds of a door slamming open and glass breaking came from the rear of the house. In the next second a man staggered into view, one arm upraised and clutching an object that glinted silver in the pale afternoon sunlight—the aluminum frame of a large-caliber automatic. Royce Smith. His red hair was like a beacon.

Griff yelled, "Smith! Drop the gun, freeze!"

Smith slowed but did not halt, half-turning in our direction. It looked to me as though he pulled the trigger on the automatic, but if so, it failed to fire. All he would have hit if it had gone off, the way his arm was bent at an upward angle, was a low-flying bird. Neither Griff nor I fired at him, though we would have been justified in doing so if he had stood his

ground and made another attempt to shoot at us. But he didn't. He spun
again and lurched away in the direction of the barn.

We gave chase. Pursuit situation now, direct pursuit of an armed and
dangerous suspect; that we were on private property without a warrant
was no longer an issue.

Ley de fuga. The odd, foolish thought came from nowhere as I ran
and vanished just as quickly. A measure of my loathing for men like
Royce Smith. But I had no wish to blow him away, would not unless
he forced me to act in self-defense. I wanted him taken alive, as I had
taken the machete-wielding mass murderer Jorge Martinez that day
long ago.

Smith ignored another shouted command to halt. He was almost to
the barn now, some thirty yards of open ground between him and us. It
was uneven ground, weed grown, and Griff stumbled as he called out,
lost his balance, sprawled headlong. I did not break stride. Smith had
reached the barn doors, was pawing at one of the halves, trying to drag
it open.

From the corner of my eye I saw Puchinsky come limping out through
the back door. "Smith!" he bellowed. "Don't go in there, you stupid shit!"

Smith ignored him, too. He had the door open now, flung himself
inside the barn.

I changed direction slightly so that I would not be in line with the
open doorway. When I reached the barn, I drew up tight against the
closed door half. A few seconds later Griff was there next to me. Puchinsky
had ceased shouting, ceased staggering forward; I saw him drop to one
knee with his head down.

I could hear Smith moving around inside, banging into unseen objects.
Then, surprisingly, light blossomed in there. I moved forward, eased my
head around the door edge for a quick scan of the interior.

The light came from one of several bulbs strung along the rafters—the
old-fashioned kind with dangling pull cords. Smith had yanked one
of the cords and was scrabbling among an arrangement of soda pop
bottles connected with rubber tubing and duct tape. He still held the
automatic, the muzzle pointed down at the floor. His movements were

jerky, confused, his face shiny with sweat and flushed almost as red as his hair. Kite high on meth. Stoned beyond reason.

Griff said in a hoarse whisper, "What's he doing?"

"Hunting for more drugs. Meth lab's in there."

"He looking this way?"

"No."

"The gun?"

"Still in his hand. Pointed at the floor."

Noise came from the yard behind us, vehicle doors slamming, then the roar of an engine. A quick glance showed me the blue Mustang fishtailing backward, its tires spinning up swirls of dust. Palumbo and at least one other person—not Puchinsky, he was still kneeling on the weedy ground. But even if they escaped the backup patrol unit on Dobler Road, they would not get far.

From inside the barn came a sudden animal-like keening, then a string of furious obscenities. Glass shattered; something metallic thumped and clattered as if it had been thrown or kicked. I poked my head around the doorjamb again. Smith's back was to the door now. He was frenziedly kicking at a pile of waste material, at the same time loosely pointing the automatic at the connected pop bottles and repeatedly jerking the trigger. The angry babbling was because the weapon refused to fire.

I pulled back long enough to say, "The gun's either jammed or empty."

"Go."

I went quick and quiet around the edge of the door into the barn, Griff close behind me and then fanning out to my left. Smith took no notice; in his drug frenzy, he seemed to have forgotten about us. He continued to kick at the waste pile, to curse the useless automatic. If he had kept that up long enough, we might have been able to move in fast and take him unawares. But before we could take more than a few steps, he hurled the gun at the pop bottles, shattering another one, and when he did that, his body and head turned and he saw me. Only me. He did not seem to notice Griff, or to hear another of the chief's shouted commands.

He swiped sweat out of his eyes, made that keening sound again, and charged me. Head down, arms extended, like an enraged bull charging a matador's red cape.

I sidestepped him as easily as a matador would have, tripped him as he went by, and sent him sprawling belly down into a stack of cat-litter bags. The fall jarred him long enough for me to drop down on top of him with my knee in his back. As small in stature as he was, he fought me with so much strength I had no choice but to stun him with the barrel of my Glock. Even then, it took both Griff and me half a minute to hold him down and cuff his hands behind his back. His legs kept thrashing, mostly in reflex now, making it necessary to bind them with a length of the rubber tubing.

Griff picked up and examined the automatic, a Colt .45. "Jammed tight. Our lucky day in more ways than one."

"For sure."

"By the book, Robert," Griff said then, nodding at Smith. "I'll get us some help. And see about Puchinsky."

I read Smith his rights, even though he was too wasted to understand them and respond. We would Mirandize him again at the station later when he was sober enough to be lucid.

Before I went outside to join Griff, I took a long look around the interior.

This was no small-scale mom-and-pop lab, but an operation large enough to supply all the addicts and would-be addicts in Santa Rita and part of the county as well. The barn was filled with the equipment and chemical products and substances, used and unused, necessary for the manufacture of methamphetamines. Hundreds of full and empty packages of medications containing ephedrine and pseudoephedrine, the primary ingredients. Volatile organic compounds such as lithium drained from batteries. Containers of ether, paint thinner, muriatic acid, alcohol. Compressed-gas cylinders. A camp stove. Coils of rubber tubing, rolls of duct tape. Bags of cat litter and Epsom salts. Holes had been drilled in the walls to ventilate the dangerous hydrogen chloride gas fumes released during the cooking. Still, it was a wonder the whole place hadn't blown up by now.

I did not see any of what Smith had been hunting for, powdered and crystallized meth ready to be swallowed, inhaled, injected, or smoked. Puchinsky would most likely have that hidden away inside the house. But we didn't need it to arrest and charge him. There was more than enough evidence right here.

GRIFFIN KELLS

WE BOOKED ROYCE SMITH on charges of attempted murder and resisting arrest, but in his stoned condition it was hours before we were able to interrogate him.

Leonard Puchinsky we booked for violation of California Health and Safety Code 11379.6 HS, the illegal manufacture of drugs, narcotics, and controlled substances. We'd had no trouble taking him into custody, though he'd turned mute immediately afterward and remained that way except for demanding a lawyer. Once he consulted with one, he refused to answer any questions that might incriminate him.

His lawyer, a young public defender, thought the DA would be unable to make the charges stick, but when I spoke to Gavin Conrad, he was confident that he could. Robert and I had been completely justified in entering the barn in pursuit of an armed and dangerous Smith, thus our discovery of the meth lab had not been the result of an illegal search; no competent trial judge was likely to rule otherwise. Judge Kiley supported our position by granting a search warrant for the farmhouse, which turned up twenty-two ounces of powdered and crystal meth stashed in a bedroom closet. The odds were good that Puchinsky would do time in one of the state lockups.

The situation with Jason Palumbo was less cut-and-dried. He and a woman companion had been stopped just after they left the farm property and held by patrol officers Chang and Gonsolves, who found no drugs on either of them or in the vehicle. They both claimed they hadn't known drugs were on the premises. All we could do was hold Palumbo temporarily as a material witness. Unless somebody was willing to testify against him—not Courtney Reeves, she had no direct knowledge that he'd been dealing—he would walk. But he was the type who wouldn't learn from a close call; it was a good bet that he'd make the mistake of hooking up with another Puchinsky, and maybe then we'd nail him too.

Smith was in bad shape when he finally sobered up—the binge he'd been on had apparently lasted for days. Shaky, sweaty, and plenty scared. Scared enough to waive his right to counsel and terrified when Robert and I listed the charges against him.

He claimed not to remember trying to shoot us with Puchinsky's .45 automatic (legally registered, surprisingly) or any of what went down inside the barn. This was probably true—a drug-induced mental block. But he couldn't get away with the same claim about raping Angela Lowenstein. Tremors racked him and his face turned a splotchy, rosacea-like red when we accused him. It didn't take much verbal hammering to break him down and get a confession.

He couldn't get her out of his mind, he said, she was like an obsession with him, but she wouldn't have anything to do with him, always acting so superior and stuck-up, then she'd left her purse in an open desk drawer when she went to the toilet and he'd taken her apartment key, but he wouldn't have done anything with it if her old man hadn't ragged on him again in front of everybody, that made him want to get back at both of them, and he knew which nights she took college classes down in Riverton because she'd mentioned it once in the office, so he'd bought the mask and gloves and knife and then got cranked up and used the key to get into her apartment, but he didn't intend to rape her, no, just scare her by pretending to be the serial rapist, but he went kind of crazy when she came home, couldn't control himself, he was sorry when he sobered up afterward, felt so bad he'd stayed wasted ever since . . . blah, blah, blah, the usual garbled, self-serving, bullshit excuses you get from stupid felons once they're in custody.

He threw a literal fit when we suggested he was guilty of the other four rapes, screaming, "No! It wasn't me, it wasn't me, only Angela, none of those other women, I swear to God it wasn't me!" On and on like that, his fear so intense a scud of froth dribbled from a corner of his mouth.

It *wasn't* him. A onetime copycat, nothing more. I knew it and so did Robert even before Smith told us where to find the mask, gloves, and knife—the damn fool had them in a closet in his apartment. Angela's key, too, still attached to the miniature dream catcher.

There could be little doubt now that the contents of the bundle found at the marina belonged to the serial. Which left us with the same still-unanswered questions.

Who had abandoned the bundle and why?

Was Martin Torrey the serial or was it somebody else?

And who had murdered Martin Torrey?

TED LOWENSTEIN

WHEN CHIEF KELLS CALLED to tell me they'd caught the man who raped Angela, and who he was, I ran the gamut of emotional reactions. Relief mixed with surprise first of all, then rage at Royce Smith, then guilt and anger at myself for not only hiring the miserable little bastard but for keeping him on staff despite his substandard journalism. It made me want to puke, thinking of him sitting at his desk ogling Angela—I'd seen him doing that, for God's sake, hadn't thought anything about it—and fantasizing and planning what he was going to do to her.

"You can't blame yourself, Daddy," Angela said when I relayed the news to her. She was sitting propped up on pillows in the living room, Tony Ciccoti beside her holding her hand. "You had no way of knowing what kind of man Royce Smith is."

"Or that he's a junkie," Tony said. "He never showed any signs of addiction when he was in the office, did he?"

"If he had, I would have fired him on the spot," I said. "But there were indications that I missed. Late arrivals at the office now and then, a couple of stories handed in late and a missed assignment. I should have realized the possibility that drugs were responsible."

"I didn't," Angela said. "Nobody else did, either."

She looked much better now that she was home, color in her cheeks, some of the old sparkle in her eyes. But she winced whenever she moved too quickly, a grim reminder of the pain she was suffering. She hadn't complained, however, not once. Brave. Strong. She would come through this all right in the long run. With emotional scars, yes, that was inevitable, but they wouldn't cripple her. She wouldn't allow that to happen.

"Are the police sure Smith isn't the one who raped those other women?" Tony asked.

"Evidently. Angela was his only victim."

"Well, I hope they throw the book at him. Put him in a maximum-security prison where he'll get done to him what he did to Angela."

"Tony, don't," Angela said. "Please."

"Sorry, honey. I can't help hating him."

Neither could I. And I couldn't help agreeing with Tony and what he had wished would happen to Smith. What was that old saw? A liberal is somebody who hasn't been mugged. Yes, or a man whose daughter hasn't been raped. Right now I had a hard time believing that vengeance is the Lord's prerogative, and that hate is a hollow emotion. I had always been a vehement opponent of capital punishment. If Royce Smith had been eligible for lethal injection, it would have been difficult for me to sustain that belief now, too.

Tony suggested we have something to eat. Angela wasn't hungry, and neither was I, but he insisted. He was a good kid. He'd stayed with Angela at the hospital most of yesterday, been here for her since she was released. If she loved him, and it seemed obvious that she did, I hoped she would marry him whether it meant a faraway move or not. My feelings had previously been somewhat selfish. Her happiness from now on was my only concern.

While Tony was in the kitchen, I received a call from Tyler James, wanting to consult on how the news of Smith's arrest was to be presented in the *Clarion*. We discussed that, then the discovery of the meth lab and arrest of Leonard Puchinsky. I told him I would write an editorial tonight praising Chief Kells and his men for their excellent work in both cases. I was ready, almost eager, to get back to work myself now.

Three more calls came in while we were having dinner on TV trays in the living room—soup and grilled-cheese sandwiches, simple fare but made with Tony's usual skill. All three calls were from well-wishers. As was a fourth, after we finished eating. All were from friends of Angela's and mine.

Before I sat down to write my editorial, I made a call of my own—to the one person I hadn't heard from, who wasn't and never would be a friend in any sense of the word.

HUGH DELAHUNT

I MUST SAY I had mixed feelings about the capture and confession of Royce Smith and the arrest of the methamphetamines dealer. The removal of dangerous criminals and the source of dangerous drugs from the streets of any city—and Santa Rita particularly—were cause for rejoicing. What made Smith's capture even more satisfying was that he had been a *Clarion* employee. A veritable viper in Ted Lowenstein's bosom, targeting the man's daughter the entire time he worked for that rag, no doubt. The fallout from this would surely harm Lowenstein's credibility in the community, and by extension the credibility of his unwarranted attacks on me.

That Smith had vehemently denied committing the previous four assaults was not as disturbing as it might have been. I still believed Martin Torrey to have been the guilty party. The inability of Kells and Ortiz to bring Torrey's murderer to justice was unfortunate, of course, but this too had its positive side where my feud with Lowenstein was concerned.

Not that I wanted those crimes to remain unsolved indefinitely. Certainly not. But the longer they were, the better the chances of convincing the council member holdouts to replace Kells and Ortiz. This might take longer than I had anticipated because of the Smith and Puchinsky arrests, but I remained optimistic that it would be accomplished eventually.

I made the mistake of voicing these thoughts to Margaret, Craig, and

Katherine over dinner. Margaret put on one of her disapproving moues and accused me of being petty and self-serving. Nonsense. I was merely being practical. I had suffered long and hard from Lowenstein's unwarranted vendetta, hadn't I? And it was in the community's best interests to replace inept police officials, despite their recent strokes of luck, with more competent, less disruptive individuals.

The four of us were having coffee and brandy in the parlor when my phone jingled. I had had two calls from the media already, and this was a third. But those first two had been welcome; this one wasn't. Ted Lowenstein. Damn. I would have preferred to duck him, but that would have been unwise under the present circumstances.

I waited to answer until I was on the way into the privacy of my study. "I was just about to call you, Ted."

"Oh, sure you were," he said in that snotty way of his.

"I was. To tell you how pleased and relieved I am that your daughter's attacker has been apprehended—"

"Bullshit."

"I beg your pardon?"

"You heard me. You don't give a flying fig about Angela or me. What pleases you is that Royce Smith worked for the *Clarion*."

"That's not true. It was as much a shock to me as I'm sure it was to you—"

"Bullshit," he said again.

"Now, Ted," I said indignantly, "you have no cause to use such language with me." I couldn't help adding, "Or to continue your public harassment, for that matter."

"Are you going to continue yours?"

"Mine? I have no idea what you mean."

"Your campaign to get rid of Griffin Kells and Robert Ortiz constitutes harassment in my book."

I stroked my mustache to give myself time to shape an appropriate response. "I believe, firmly and justifiably, that there are men who are better qualified—"

"Yes-men. Toadies. Ass kissers."

"Now listen here. Just because Kells and Ortiz were lucky enough to catch your daughter's rapist and close down a drug operation—"

"Luck had nothing to do with it. Good police work did."

"If they are such skilled officers, why are the serial assaults still an open case? Why is Martin Torrey's murderer still at large?"

"Lack of necessary evidence."

"Proper effort provides necessary evidence."

"That's right. Proper effort put Smith and Puchinsky behind bars. Sooner or later it will put the rapist, if he's not already dead, and Torrey's killer in there with them."

"'Sooner or later' is unacceptable."

"To you and your agenda."

"I have no agenda, as you put it—"

Lowenstein laughed, nastily. "So you intend to go on pushing the council to fire Kells."

"Yes, for the reasons I just told you."

"Then you can expect my support to be twice as strong as before. My so-called harassment of you and your administration, likewise. All within strict legal boundaries, of course."

"I'm warning you, Lowenstein—"

"No, I'm warning *you*. You know what you are, Mayor, you and all the politicians just like you?"

I had no desire to have that question answered, so I held my tongue. But he answered it anyway, in even more detestable terms.

"Vampire bats," he said.

". . . What?"

"You heard me. Bloodsuckers that care only about feeding themselves, that foul the public nest while feathering their own. Mixed metaphor, but apt just the same."

"How dare you—!"

"The longer one of your breed survives and the higher it flies, the more damage it does. I won't stand by and watch you get any more bloated than you already are, foul any more nests. Oh, hell, no. I'm going to see to it that you're no longer a threat here or anywhere else in this state. I'm going to build a sharp journalistic stake and drive it through your black heart. That's not a threat, it's a promise."

He ended the call with that. I sat there, shaken. The man was mad, a stark raving lunatic. Vampire bat . . . journalistic stake through my heart . . . good God!

Let him mount a scurrilous attack on me in print. People would see it for what it was, an attempted character assassination—the vicious ramblings of a diseased mind. None of my backers in the party would take him seriously. Neither would the voters. Of course they wouldn't. That miserable little prick couldn't possibly succeed in destroying my plans, my future.

Could he?

ROBERT ORTIZ

A FTER TEN O'CLOCK MASS on Sunday morning I drove Sofia and
the girls home and apologized once again for abandoning them on
the Sabbath.

Sofia said, "Please, Roberto, you know we understand. You must do
your job. *Gracias estén a Dios* that you and Chief Kells were not harmed
yesterday—that is what is important."

I had not told her all the details of the incidents at the Puchinsky
farm. We had no secrets from each other, but some things, those that
needlessly frighten loved ones, are better left unspoken. "This summer,"
I said, "we'll finally take the family vacation you have all been asking for."

Daniela put her cell phone aside long enough to say, "Oh, Papa, you
mean a trip to Disneyland?"

"To Disneyland, yes."

"All the rides, all the attractions? That'll take at least a week."

"Everything there is to see and do."

"Promise?"

"Promise." It was one I would keep, no matter what happened between
now and then.

I drove to the station. The latest media infestation had eased; I did not
have to answer or dodge questions before or after I entered, fortunately.
Griff had not come in yet, though he was expected.

There was a stack of reports on my desk. The first I looked at confirmed that the mask, gloves, and knife used by Royce Smith had been recovered from his apartment closet, along with a small amount of marijuana. No methamphetamines; he had long ago abused his central nervous system with whatever supply he might have had. The evidence had all been tagged and checked into the property room. Later it would be examined by Joe Bloom, then sent to Ed Braverman for forensic tests.

The report on the suicide of Eileen Jordan was a grim reminder of how vital it was to bring closure to the serial investigation. Perhaps the schoolteacher would have taken her life if we had already succeeded, but I could not help but feel we were partly responsible. That we had failed her, and failed the other three victims as well.

Joe Bloom had finished his preliminary analysis of the bundle that had been found at the marina. The serial's tools, no question of that now. The knife bore no identifying marks of any kind, and the handle had been wiped clean. Braverman's tests of the blood residue on the blade would surely produce a DNA match with one or more of the assault victims. The gloves and ski mask were of ordinary and inexpensive manufacture, the kind that can be bought in any sporting goods or chain department store. The cloth they had been wrapped in was a plain white dish towel, also of ordinary manufacture.

One potentially helpful fact was the nature of the oily residues on the towel. There were two types. One, in trace quantities, was a lubricant used to clean firearms. This indicated that the .38-caliber weapon stolen from the Spivey home may have been stored with the other items at one time. Why it had not been discarded as well had several possible answers, all of them speculative.

The other type of residue existed in much greater quantity. Ninety-eight percent mineral oil, the other two percent unspecified friction modifiers and lubricity agents. I had no idea what that sort of oil compound was used for. And it was not explained in the report.

Joe Bloom's wife answered my call to his cell. Yes, he was home, preparing for a backyard barbecue they were hosting. She went to fetch him.

"Don't tell me we have another crisis to deal with," he said when he came on the line.

"No. I have a question."

"Well, that's a relief. Maybe I'll actually get to have a pleasant Sunday off. What's the question?"

"I've just been reading your report on the oil residue on the towel. Friction modifiers and lubricity agents mixed with mineral oil. What would that compound be used for?"

"Only one thing I know of. Didn't I put it in the report?"

"No."

"Sorry, I meant to. I worked late last night and I guess I must've spaced out toward the end."

"What is it used for, Joe?"

"Conditioner for bowling lanes."

"Bowling lanes," I repeated.

"Right. I looked it up on the net. The mineral oil allows the balls—urethane coverstock, reactive resin, whatever they're made of—to roll smoothly, and the additives regulate the viscosity, which in turn controls friction and the amount of hook and spin you can put on the ball."

"And the towel's original purpose?"

"My guess is it's a bowler's towel, used to wipe the ball between rolls to remove excess oil from the lanes."

I sat for some minutes after we disconnected, thinking, remembering, shaping an idea. Then again I picked up my phone.

IONE SPIVEY

I WAS CLEANING OUT the kitchen cabinets, putting down new shelf paper, when the telephone rang. The cabinets didn't need cleaning, any more than the floors had needed scrubbing or the pantry rearranging or the closets reorganizing, but busywork helps steady my nerves and keep my mind occupied. I'd done a lot of it these past few days. And I'd do more today, even though it was Sunday. All because of that god-awful assault rifle or whatever it is.

Jack took it today to that ranch he'd told me about to practice firing it. And took Timmy with him. He wouldn't listen when I tried to talk him out of it, any more than he had when I tried to talk him out of stock-piling more of the damn things. I'd talked until I was blue in the face about how dangerous it was to have weapons like that in the house, to let a ten-year-old boy shoot one, and he wouldn't listen to that, either. Once Jack gets an idea in his head, you couldn't get it out with a pry bar. He's stubborn, hotheaded, foolish sometimes, but he's never done anything to make me regret I married him or to frighten me so until now.

It was Timmy I was worried about. He idolizes his father, to the point of being a mirror image of him. It wasn't that I was afraid he'd grow up to be the kind of man Jack was, I was afraid he wouldn't—that he'd grow up to be somebody I didn't want to be my son.

I couldn't get the picture out of my mind of him holding and pointing that assault weapon. The look in his eyes, the almost sexual excitement . . . my Lord! Jack didn't notice it, thinks I imagined it. Timmy's just a boy, he says, lots of boys are fascinated by guns, it's no big deal. But it *is* a big deal. What happens when Timmy is old enough to move out on his own, live his life without any supervision? What happens if his passion for guns becomes an obsession and he doesn't have the same self-governing on his actions that Jack does?

The phone ringing was a welcome distraction, or it was until I heard Lieutenant Ortiz's voice. It put another scare into me because the first thing I thought of was that Jack and Timmy had been caught with that assault gun, arrested. But thank heaven that wasn't why he was calling.

He asked if Jack was home, and when I told him no, he said, "You may be able to help me, Mrs. Spivey. This may sound like an odd question, but I have a good reason for asking. Where does your husband keep his bowling equipment?"

". . . His bowling equipment? You mean ball, bag, shoes?"

"Yes. At home, in his vehicle?"

"Neither. In a locker at Santa Rita Lanes, so he doesn't have to carry them back and forth."

"A locker."

"You know, like the ones they used to have in bus depots. Some league bowlers rent them, they're not expensive."

"How are they opened? With a combination lock or a key?"

"A key, I think."

"One with a small red dot on it?"

"Red dot? I'm not sure, you'd have to ask my husband . . ."

"That won't be necessary," he said, and thanked me and hung up.

I stood holding the phone for a few seconds before I put it down. Now what on earth was that all about?

LIANE TORREY

O RTIZ AGAIN. I OPENED the door and there he was alone on the porch, big and grim looking as always.

"I know about the man you arrested yesterday," I said before he could say anything. "Are you here to tell me he's responsible for all the rapes?"

"No. Only the last one."

"Then what is it you want?"

"Another look inside your garage."

"The garage? What for?"

"Do you object, Mrs. Torrey?"

"No. Why should I? Go ahead."

"I'd like you to come with me."

I was too weary, too discouraged, to argue. I shrugged and walked out there with him. Inside the garage, he led me around the Subaru to the catchall bench on the far wall.

"You cleaned out some of what was here before," he said.

"I didn't think I needed permission to give Martin's belongings to a charity shop."

"That depends on what you gave away."

Ortiz walked alongside the bench, bent over at the waist to peer underneath. At the upper end he squatted and dragged out one of the few remaining boxes, the one with Martin's bowling ball and shoes in it.

"I saw these when I was here last week," he said.

"I doubted anyone would want them."

He ran his finger over the surface of the ball, over one of the shoes. "Dusty. How long have they been here?"

"A while. Since Martin lost interest in bowling."

"When was that?"

"After he quit the Soderholm team last year."

"He hadn't been bowling since?"

"No. Not that I know of."

"Why are his ball and shoes stored loose like this, instead of in a bag?"

"I don't know. He never said why he left them here like that."

"Did he have a bag to carry them in back then?"

"I guess so. Yes."

"What happened to it?"

"I don't know," I said again. "I never thought to ask."

"Do you know if he rented a locker when he was with the team?"

"He never said anything about a locker. Why are you asking all these questions?"

"To get at the truth, Mrs. Torrey. Finally, after all this time."

"What truth? What are you talking about?"

But he wouldn't tell me. He went away and left me with a bad feeling— the kind of feeling I'd had the first time I set eyes on him.

No. One that was even worse.

ROBERT ORTIZ

SANTA RITA LANES WAS located at one end of a large, fairly new shopping center on Hillsdale Avenue. I parked in its lot and entered the place for the first time in my life. Several of the lanes were in use, the crash and clatter of balls rolling and pins toppling loud in my ears. A middle-aged woman presided over the desk where lanes and shoes were rented. I showed her my badge, told her why I was there.

There were thirty-six lockers in an alcove next to the manager's office, she said, and yes, the keys all had small red dots. The establishment was not responsible for them; the company that manufactured the lockers made the keys that way, probably as a trademark. She had no authority to let me see a list of renters' names. I had to wait while she phoned the manager for his permission to bring up the list on the computer. Fortunately, he was spending his Sunday at home and proved cooperative.

With his permission, the woman looked up the locker rentals list on the main desk computer. Number 32 had been rented to Martin Torrey on October 19 of last year.

As I followed her to the alcove where the lockers were located, I wished again that I had paid more attention to Martin Torrey's red-dot key when I'd first noticed it on his key ring. Such a key is unusual, and we had not found anything incriminating at his house or in his Camry; he had to keep his rapist's tools somewhere safe and accessible, and that usually meant under lock and key. With some imaginative police work I might have found out three weeks ago what that key opened. He would not be dead if I had; he would be in jail awaiting trial on four counts of criminal assault. And Angela Lowenstein might not have been brutalized by Royce Smith.

But it was foolish and spurious to blame myself. How could I have made the connection between the key and the game of bowling without the towel and Joe Bloom's analysis of the oil residue? I had never bowled in my life. Valentina is the only member of our family who has, a time or two on one of her frequent dates. Griff Kells is not a bowler, nor is anyone on the IU. Some in the department surely are, but I had had no cause to consult any of the rank-and-file officers about the missing key. Nor was the existence of the lockers common knowledge in the community. There were only thirty-six, which meant but a few of the many league bowlers chose to rent one. Most of those who bowled for recreation likely did not even know of their existence, much less that they were opened with a red-dot key.

The manager, in addition to granting permission for Torrey's locker to be opened, had authorized me to take possession of whatever it contained. But this was not necessary.

I knew even before the woman unlocked number 32 with a passkey that the locker would be empty.

HOLLY DEXTER

WHEN I GOT OFF the phone, I went out to see Nick in his work-shop. He spends most of his Sundays in there, not that I mind unless the weather is nice and we can be out in the fresh air doing something together. Woodworking is his only hobby besides sports. I have to admit he's good at it—he's made a highboy, tables, a few other things for the house that are as good as any you'd buy at Macy's.

"I'm going over to see Liane for a while," I said.

He shut off the noisy power saw he was using and rubbed a chubby arm across his sweaty forehead. "Why?"

"I just talked to her and she sounded funny, in the doldrums again. She wouldn't say why. I'll be back in time for dinner."

"Okay. Get me a beer before you leave, will you?"

"What am I, your slave?"

"Come on, Holly. I'm in the middle of this job and it's thirsty work."

"Oh, all right."

I went back into the house and opened a Coors and took it out to him. He was sawing something and didn't even notice when I set the can down on the bench, much less thank me. That was Nick for you. Off in his own little world half the time, no real interest in me or my problems. Not much help in this family crisis of ours, either. Allan Zacks cared more about Liane than Nick did.

I backed the pickup out of the driveway, grinding the gears on purpose when I shifted from reverse into low. He probably wouldn't have heard if he was still running that rackety saw. If he did, he'd grumble about it when I came home and I'd play innocent like I always did. Sometimes he brought out the worst in me.

Down at the end of the block, just as I was passing through the intersection, a police car came up to the stop sign on Maple and then turned onto our street behind me. I only had a glimpse of the driver, but it might have been that annoying lieutenant, Ortiz. Well, if it was and he was coming to bother me again, he was out of luck. Nick could deal with him this time.

ROBERT ORTIZ

THE DRIVEWAY AT THE Dexter home was empty and no one answered the doorbell. But as I came down off the porch, I heard a muted buzzing noise from the direction of the detached garage—a power tool of some kind. It drew me along a side path to the driveway. The buzzing was somewhat louder there, coming from behind the closed garage doors.

I followed the driveway to a side door that stood a few inches ajar. The buzzing stopped just after I pushed the door open and stepped inside. Nicholas Dexter was alone in a section at the rear that had been converted into a home workshop. He had been working at a table saw, the source of the noise, evidently cutting and shaping a section of wood for a piece of furniture he was making; now he stood with his head tipped back, drinking from a can of beer. He did not see me until he lowered the can, by which time I was halfway across the oil-stained concrete floor.

He blinked several times, reaching back to set the can down on the workbench. "Oh . . . Lieutenant. Gave me a start there."

"I would have knocked before I came in, but you wouldn't have heard me."

"No problem. Holly's not home if you're here to see her—"

"No, Mr. Dexter, it's you I came to see."

"Oh? Well. What can I do for you?"

I moved ahead to stand in front of him, the table saw between us.

The workshop area radiated warmth from an electric space heater. The mingled odors of new wood and sawdust, linseed oil, furniture stain, might have been pleasant at some other time, in some other place.

"You can tell me why you lied to me."

"Why I . . . what?" He blinked again. "I never lied to you."

"I think you did."

"What would I lie about?"

I said, "You bowl regularly, is that right?"

The question confused him, as I had intended it should. "Bowl? What does bowling have to do with anything?"

"A great deal. You've been with the Soderholm Brewery team in the same Tuesday-night mixed league for several years. Seven, to be exact."

"I guess that's how many, sure, but—"

"And all that time you've rented the same locker. Number twenty-one."

The expression on his round face altered, his gaze shifting away from mine. "That's right."

"Seven years. The same locker, the same locker key."

"So?"

"I have been told all the locker keys have red dots on them, every one issued to renters since Santa Rita Lanes opened. That means yours has one. But when I asked you last week about a silver key with a red dot, you told me you'd never seen one."

"I told you I'd never seen the one Marty had . . ."

"No. 'I've never seen one anywhere'—your exact words."

"I . . . I never pay any attention to what keys look like . . ."

"One you've had for seven years and use at least once a week? I find that very hard to believe."

He blinked again and shook his head, a reflexive movement.

"Your brother-in-law also rented a locker when he joined the Soderholm team last year. But when he quit after three weeks, he retained the locker. Number thirty-two."

". . . What's wrong with that? Some bowlers keep their equipment at the lanes even if they're not in leagues. Marty liked to bowl, he just didn't like being on a team."

"He bowled often then, did he?"

"Not often. Now and then."

"With you?"

"By himself mostly. But sometimes, yeah, I'd go with him. You know, just for fun."

"His wife told me he hadn't bowled at all since quitting the team."

"She did?" Dexter half-turned to pick up the beer can, took a long swallow from it. "Well . . . she's wrong. Marty didn't tell her everything . . ."

"Did he keep his equipment in his locker?"

"I guess so. That's what it's for."

"Then why have his ball and shoes been in a carton in his garage for several months, gathering dust? What happened to his bag?"

"I . . . I don't . . ."

"And why is his locker empty now?"

I counted silently to eight before he said, "I don't know. How should I know?"

"You've lied to me twice now, Mr. Dexter. What are you hiding?"

"I'm not hiding anything, I . . ."

"Whoever emptied his locker must have used his key. Was it you?"

"No. I never had his key."

"You didn't remove his bowling bag from inside?"

"No. I just told you . . ."

"And then take the contents to the North Park Marina and leave them under one of the benches?"

Dexter's face had lost color, become pinched and creased like unkneaded tortilla dough. Tiny bubbles of sweat had popped out on his forehead. "What contents?"

"A bundle wrapped in a bowling towel."

"No, no! Why would I do a crazy thing like that?"

I said, "Friday night, April sixteenth."

". . . What?"

"The night Martin Torrey was shot to death in Echo Park."

"What about it? I told that other cop I was home watching a ball game that night . . ."

"You didn't go out even for a few minutes?"

"No. Stayed in the house the whole evening."

"Then one of your neighbors couldn't possibly have noticed your pickup leaving or returning."

He jerked as if I'd struck him. "What neighbor?"

I said nothing, watching him.

"Somebody told you that," Dexter said, "he's wrong or he's lying."

"What reason would a neighbor have to lie?"

"How the hell should I know? You keep mixing me up, accusing me . . ."

"I haven't accused you of anything except lying to me, twice."

"You think I killed Marty. That's what this is all about, isn't it?"

"*Did* you kill him?"

"No! Why would I? The miserable son of a bitch owed me fifteen hundred dollars . . ."

"Miserable son of a bitch, Mr. Dexter? I thought you and your brother-in-law were friends, close friends."

"Close? Nobody ever got close to Marty."

"Then you weren't friends."

"I didn't say that . . ."

"Why did you call him a miserable son of a bitch?"

"Because he was. Because he . . ."

"Because he what? Because he was the serial rapist and you knew it?"

"I didn't know it, not until—"

He'd said too much, and when he realized it, a panicked look spread over his doughy features. His head swiveled from side to side and then held still, his eyes on a hammer that lay on the workbench. I moved around the end of the table saw, opening my coat and resting my hand on the butt of the Glock. When he saw me do that, he stiffened and the panic ebbed. He had nowhere to go. Would have had nowhere to go even if he weren't trapped behind the table saw, hemmed in by it and the bench on two sides, a lathe behind him, me in front of him. His shoulders sagged; he leaned heavily against the table. If it had not been there, I thought, his legs would not have continued to support his weight.

"Martin Torrey raped those four women, didn't he," I said.

". . . Yeah. Yeah, he raped them."

"And you murdered him because of it."

"No." His voice, now, was a hoarse whisper. "I didn't murder him, it wasn't murder."

"You're lying again—"

"I'm not lying," Dexter said. "The sick bastard killed himself. All I did was pull the trigger for him."

NICHOLAS DEXTER

M Y NAME IS NICHOLAS Henry Dexter. I live at 1427 Stover Street, Santa Rita. I have been advised of my rights, waived my right to presence of counsel, and make this statement voluntarily and with full understanding that it may be used against me in a court of law.

All right. This is the way it was.

That Friday night, April 15, Marty called me on my cell about a quarter of eight, right after Holly picked up Liane for their movie date. He knew I had no plans for the evening except to watch a ball game on TV; I guess Holly must've said something to Liane and she passed it on to him. He said he had something very important to tell me, but not at my house or his, it had to be someplace else. I asked him why; he said he had his reasons. Closemouthed, like he always was. He wanted me to meet him on South Street, down near the railroad yards, at eight thirty. It sounded funny . . . that's a pretty deserted area on a weekend night. He wouldn't say why there, just that he'd explain when he saw me.

Well, I didn't want to go. But he was my brother-in-law, and he kept saying how important it was, and I couldn't help being curious . . . so finally I said okay. He was waiting when I got down there at eight thirty. Right away he locked up his car and got into my pickup, but he wouldn't talk there either. Drive to Echo Park, he said, then he'd tell me what was so important. I asked him why Echo Park? He wouldn't tell me that, either.

I tried to pump him on the way, but he just kept saying, when we get there, Nick, when we get there. He told me to stop on Parkside across from the park, in a space in the line of cars parked there, then when the street was empty he said Come with me, Nick and got out and ran across into the park. What else could I do but follow him? There was a sort of path where he went into the trees and we walked along that until we came out on that riverbank. He sat down on a bench on the path that comes over from the picnic grounds, and I sat down with him, and that was when he told me, there in the dark so I couldn't see his face, that he was the one who raped those women.

A sick compulsion he couldn't control, he said, like the one he'd had back in Ohio, only ten times worse because now he had to do things to the women, not just yank his shank while he watched them through windows. Said he hated himself for that and for thoughts he was having now about not just raping another woman but maybe killing her this time. All of this in a flat voice, no emotion, like he was talking about baseball or something.

Jesus, you can imagine how blown away I was. All the time I believed he was innocent, same as Liane and Holly did. It made me want to puke sitting there in the dark listening to this crazy shit. And mad as hell and about half-nuts, too. I never liked Marty very much and right then I hated him, I mean I really *hated* the son of a bitch. My first impulse was to clobber him, then I wanted to run back to my pickup and go straight to the police station. But I didn't do either. I just kept on sitting there.

Why confess to me? I said. Why not go to the cops and tell them? No, he said, he couldn't stand to be locked up in prison or another loony bin. He'd rather die, he said. He'd given it a lot of thought and that was what he wanted, what he had to do—die before he gave in to the compulsion again. Then why don't you just off yourself? I said.

That was when he showed me the gun.

At first I was scared. Hell, who wouldn't be in a situation like that? But all he did was hold it in his hand and start talking again, saying it was the gun he'd stolen after he raped Jack Spivey's wife, saying he'd tried to use it on himself half a dozen times but he couldn't do it, he didn't have the guts. "I need you to do it for me, Nick," he said. That was the reason he'd brought me down there, opened up to me the way he had. I was the only person he could turn to, he said, the only person who could put him out of his misery and protect Liane at the same time. Not just asking me to shoot him, the way he said it. Telling me I had to. Ordering me to do it.

That was as much of a shock as him confessing. Worse. It scrambled up my thinking. I mean, I didn't know what to do or say. I should have gotten up then and run like hell, but I couldn't seem to move. He had me and he knew it, knew how much I hated him now that I knew what he'd done to those women. Knew it from the get-go. Knew me better than I knew myself.

He had the whole thing planned down to the last detail. He said the knife and mask and gloves he'd used were in his bowling bag, and the bag was in his locker at the lanes. He said the locker key was in his coat pocket. Wait a couple of days, he said, then get the bag, take the bundle that was inside, and put it someplace where somebody would find it and turn it over to the police. That way, with him dead and no more rapes, it would look like the rapist had dumped the stuff and left town. And Liane would never have to know the truth about him. Holly, neither. No one, ever, but me.

Crazy. Crazy man, crazy plan.

But he didn't give me any time to think about it. He got up and walked down the bank, saying Come on, Nick, come on, so I got up and went after him. And when we were close to the river he shoved the goddamn gun in my hand, then laid down on the grass with his arms spread out and his ankles crossed . . . some kind of weird penance position or something, I don't know, like he was getting ready to ask God for forgiveness. God? Straight to hell was where he was going.

What he said then was I should kneel down and put the muzzle against his temple and pull the trigger. "Just do it, Nick. Do it for Liane, do it for Holly, do it for all those women I hurt, do it for yourself. Do it do it do it."

So I did it.

I hated him and I wanted him dead and I shot him, just like he knew I would. I thought my hand would shake so much I'd have trouble pulling the trigger, but it didn't and I didn't. Rock steady the whole time. But I was glad it was so dark. If I'd had to look at what the bullet did to his head, the blood . . .

Those two rounds into his groin was his idea, not mine. When he laid down on the grass he said make it look like some stranger did it. Oh, yeah, he had that planned, too. So I blew his brains out and then I blew his pecker and his gonads off. Then I threw the gun as far out into the river as I could. And then I took the locker key and his cell phone out of his coat pocket and went back to my car and drove home.

I went ahead and did the rest of what he'd told me to do because it was the only way I could protect myself and Holly, not just Liane. That was how I figured it, anyhow. The next day I smashed his cell and mine, both a couple of cheap prepays, and dumped the pieces in the garbage. I waited longer than he told me to before I took the goddamn bowling bag out of his locker because I was afraid of getting caught with the evidence inside. I thought about leaving the knife and other crap in the bag and throwing it all away in a Dumpster, but what if somebody found it and turned it in and the cops figured out the bag belonged to Marty? So I got rid of the bundle just like he told me to, where it'd be sure to be found, and then trashed the empty bag. If I'd done that sooner, maybe the Lowenstein girl wouldn't have been raped by that drugged-up reporter. I don't know. I feel bad about her, same as those other poor women.

But I didn't feel bad that night or since about Marty dying the way he did. I figured we'd both done the town a favor, the world a favor. Like I told Lieutenant Ortiz, I didn't really murder him, he killed himself. Me . . . I was just the method, the instrument, like the gun.

The only thing I regret is that now Liane will have to know the truth. Holly, too. But the main thing, the important thing, is that my sick damned brother-in-law will never hurt anybody else again.

GRIFFIN KELLS

Aᴺᴰ ꜱᴏ ɪᴛ'ꜱ ꜰɪɴᴀʟʟʏ finished.

Four and a half months of a rapist's reign of terror compounded by a homicide and then a copycat assault, and suddenly, in a span of two days, everything comes together in a speed rush.

It happens that way sometimes in police work. The right wheels are in motion all along, wheels within wheels, but moving so slowly you're not sure they'll ever get you anywhere. Then circumstances contrive to start the wheels spinning fast. They say things come in threes. That goes for breaks, too. Catch one, catch a second, catch a third, in rapid succession.

Yet you can't help thinking that you should have been able to make at least some of it happen sooner. Robert had had Martin Torrey correctly pegged weeks ago; if we'd pushed Torrey harder despite the lack of evidence, we might have gotten him to slip up, to confess. We'd had sufficient information to piece together the answers to his murder, too, if we hadn't been wed to the wrong assumptions about the motive, hadn't let all the oddities and inconsistencies—the Echo Park location, the position of the body, the groin shots, the abandoned Camry—cloud the issue.

But then you think, no, you and Robert and the IU team did as much as any small-town officers with limited resources could reasonably be expected to. The crimes were too carefully planned and executed, too confusing, to be quickly and easily resolved. Even in this day and age, with all the electronic and forensic tools at law enforcement's disposal, apprehending felons can take weeks, months, even years. And sometimes it can't be done at all. All too often perps of every sort of crime remain unidentified, go unpunished.

What bothered me most of all, and would for a long time, were the dark consequences of the crimes. They hadn't been, couldn't be, erased by the solutions—the pain and sorrow, the bitter regret, the physical and mental damage so many had suffered at the hands of Martin Torrey, Royce Smith, even Nicholas Dexter. Not only the four women Torrey had violated and the one, Eileen Jordan, he had condemned to death as surely as he had condemned himself. Members of their immediate families, their friends. Angela Lowenstein. Ted Lowenstein. Liane Torrey. Holly Dexter. All violated in one way or another; all with wounds that for some might never heal.

When I got home late that night and shared all of this with Jenna, she said, "You left yourself and Robert off the list, Griff."

"Neither of us was hurt anywhere near as badly as the others."

"Badly enough. None of us came through this unscathed."

"You're right. Everyone involved, directly or indirectly, paid a price. Including you."

"Yes. But there are compensations for us."

"Such as?"

"You still have your job, for one."

"Well, there is that. Delahunt won't be able to get rid of me now." I smiled a little. "For that matter, if Ted Lowenstein has his way, it'll be Delahunt and his bunch who are hung out to dry."

"Let's hope so. But that's not the only positive, for you or for me. I've learned some things about myself, how selfish I've been."

"You're not selfish, Jenna."

"I was. Not anymore." She took my hand, held it between hers. "I've known about this for some time, but I didn't tell you before because I couldn't make up my mind what to do about it. Now I have. The right decision to make both of us happy."

"What're you talking about?"

"I'm pregnant," she said.

A NOTE ON THE AUTHOR

Bill Pronzini is the author of more than eighty novels, including several in collaboration with his wife, the novelist Marcia Muller, and is the creator of the popular Nameless Detective series. A six-time nominee for the Edgar Allan Poe Award (most recently for *A Wasteland of Strangers*), Pronzini is the recipient of three Shamus Awards. He received the coveted Grand Master Award from the Mystery Writers of America in May 2008. He and his wife live in Northern California.